TWISTED MAGIC CASTING

THE WITCH OF HENBANE ISLAND
BOOK 9

POPPY BRIDGEMAN

Ebook ISBN: 978-1-997949-00-8
Paperback ISBN: 978-1-997949-01-5

Cover created by Getcovers

FREE BOOK

Use the QR code to Claim your copy of Magic Will Out when you sign up for my newsletter and follow Cossi as she seeks answers to her past.

1

It didn't take long for us to find our new protectors. Or rather, for someone to call and tell Mrs. V where they were. Within a week, Kendra Walsh arrived. She was from the same Vancouver community I'd rescued the Reeves family from last year.

Yesterday, her parents brought her to the island and settled her in at The Inner Spell—the tents were gone and we were back to a retreat.

The other witch was Henry Curtis. He had a job as a librarian in a plain human library. He was joining us today.

The difference between thirteen-year-old Kendra and fifty-four-year-old Henry was going to make things interesting. Unless Henry also spent most of his time staring at his phone and pronouncing things as either awesome or totally sus, that is.

Mrs. V assured me that helping a real protector find their feet was very different from trying to train people without the power. Perhaps I'd done such a bad job last week, the universe decided to awaken the powers after a long period. Although maybe I should think of myself as the first of the new protectors? I let that thought go to the very back of my mind.

"If you are the first, and you are my familiar, then you should use the power you have," Destroyer, my crow familiar, said. "Emperors are required to rule."

I didn't need his two cents. "I need to focus on my students."

"I will be here when you realize I am needed for you to be successful."

I didn't respond. It wouldn't change his imperial mind, and since his army had come through in the last case, I didn't want to seem ungrateful.

The morning was a normal one on Henbane. Other than seasonal changes, most days I woke to birds singing and a fresh breeze. It sounds boring, but it wasn't. There was a peace to be found in reliability. Between learning and solving murders, my days were interesting enough.

Now, here I was, waiting for Kendra to join me in the kitchen; Jan's breakfast waited on the counter. The keep-warm spell would last for hours, so it wouldn't go bad. I wouldn't wait that long because I was starving. If she didn't show up in ten minutes, I'd eat mine and linger over my coffee. I'd hoped to show her Henbane, but nothing would formally start until Henry arrived.

I was reaching for my plate when she wandered in through the door. She flicked a glance around and said hi before looking back at her phone. Dressed in black tights and a tee-shirt emblazoned with the members of the K-pop band Black Pink. I could tell she wanted to be seen as a rebel, but the baby blue bunny slippers diminished her edginess.

"Are you hungry?" Teenagers hadn't changed that much, right? They were always hungry.

Kendra put her phone down on the counter and looked around the room. Her face was unreadable, which might help her in the role of protector. "It's real quiet here," she finally said as she picked up the coffee pot. "It's weird not to hear all the background noises. What's for breakfast?"

Not exactly rude, but I reminded myself she'd been through a huge life change. And I wasn't exactly the icon of manners. "There's a variety in the bag on the counter. Jan supplied this morning, but we'll probably do some of our own cooking while you're here."

I took a ham and egg sandwich and refilled my coffee. I could cook in a pinch, but Jan was a kitchen witch; no one could compete with that kind of magic. Since any food prepared on Henbane was healthy, I didn't need to worry about sodium or trans fats.

"So when do we start with this training? My mom said it's new and I should be grateful that I got torn away from my friends to come." She stuffed a bite into her mouth and I had the weird flash of frustration from her. She hadn't planned to say anything like that. I don't remember that being part of the protector job.

"Believe me I know how hard it is to leave your life behind," I said. "Maybe it will only be temporary. It's not like we've got protector positions open. They go where they're needed. Maybe your friends will visit. They are all witches, right?"

"And this other old guy? He's working at a plain human job. If he gets called on protector business, that's a problem."

The disconnect between what I saw in her emotions—hope, excitement, and pride—and her tone of resentment was dizzying.

"It's something we have to talk about," I said. I was not

going to be drawn into the conversation about the small details until we had a good grounding. "What are you expecting?"

She reached for another sandwich and offered to refill my coffee. It was all a delaying tactic. Her phone screen lit up behind her. She'd left it on the counter and ignored it. I was grateful I wouldn't be competing for her attention—or acting the adult and telling her to put it away.

"Mrs. Vestum," Kendra said, keeping her eyes on the plate. "She's like a Yoda kind of thing right?"

"She's been a protector the longest," I said, fighting the urge to mess with my syntax to impersonate the character. "We look to her for advice, but I see her as more of a mix of Gandalf and the wicked witch of the east."

"My mom said she could be mean and not to take it personally."

"Your mom is pretty smart." I needed Kendra to be more open about Mrs. V, or she might not learn anything. "When I got here first, I thought she hated me. She can be very grumpy but it's all about protecting our world. Think about how you would feel if that was your job and no new protectors were being born."

Kendra sipped her coffee and grimaced—maybe she just took it to look more adult. She did think about my question, so not a lost cause.

"I guess I'd be scared. And sometimes when people are scared they get mean. Is she going to yell at me if I do something wrong?"

I thought about how many times Tulip, Mrs. V's lynx familiar, tried to threaten me. At least Kendra wouldn't know about that. "No. Mrs. V doesn't yell. She's strict and has high expectations. If it gets hard, let me know." I don't know what I'd do, but a scared protector was of no use.

She turned her mug in circles and didn't look at me when she asked, "will I get a familiar?"

I guess the question didn't come as a surprise. It was pretty common for witches to want one, but the animal chose, not the witch.

"I don't know. Maybe." Henbane was just the place for it to happen.

"I will survey my empire for likely candidates," Destroyer announced. "Two familiars would be appropriate for two protectors."

"I'd like a puppy," Kendra said. "A dog can go with me when I'm traveling. So when does the other guy get here?"

2

Henry was coming from Powell River, so he had a ferry to catch before arriving at Sechelt. Thankfully, D had some errands on the mainland, so he was happy to wait and bring my second student over to Henbane.

"This afternoon," I said. "We don't have to wait around, D will let me know when he leaves the mainland. We'll have plenty of time to get to the dock and greet him. We'll start officially tomorrow when we're all together, with discussions and questions. For today, is there something you'd like to do or see?"

She glanced again at her phone. I saw the struggle to avoid it in her emotions. I kept quiet. If she wanted to spend time online, I wouldn't argue. Being a teenager was hard enough without the burden of protecting the magical world.

"Are you going to show us around the island tomorrow? Meet other witches? Can I look at the wards?" She slumped in her chair after the stream of questions as if she expected to be shut down.

"Yes. This isn't going to be all lessons, in fact, we'll be

discussing more teaching about being a protector, mostly because I think it's about using your powers rather than learning new skills. There'll be some spell work, mostly with Mrs. V because you'll need a wide range of magic."

She straightened a little as she relaxed. The purple anxiety thinned out in her aura, and I think she accepted I wasn't going to boss her around. And that maybe she could do the job.

"We can still go now," I said. "The wards aren't much to look at, but you'll get more out of it than I did. You've got a boundary power. And I didn't know I was a witch until a day before I arrived."

She stood, collected the wrappings from breakfast, and cleared the table. "Can we go now? What did you feel when you saw the wards? Can we meet some shifters? I haven't seen one before. Will your familiar come? Is it far?"

"Let's see. Yes, only a feeling of safety, yes, we'll have lunch at Sheena's. It's not far, and Destroyer does as he wants."

THE WARDS WERE in the center of the island. I assumed it was because they radiated a circle of protection. A clearing in the trees down a narrow path, way too tight for the bikes, held a circular hut. Not exactly for security, but to hold a stay-away spell for the animals.

"Shouldn't it be more... I don't know solid?" Kendra asked as she pulled twigs from her hair from brushing against the trees. "Does everyone know it's here?"

"The wards don't really need protection at all," I said. "When they first went into place, none of the witches were sure about the wildlife, so they kept them out to be safe. My familiar tells me the animals and birds know not the touch them."

Destroyer put it differently, labeling it high treason to disturb the wards. "They're buried, so you won't see the actual spells."

I watched as she moved slowly toward the opening. This was a good opportunity to assess her respect for the world. She closed her eyes before entering. A smile grew as she waited for something I couldn't feel. Her aura smoothed out into one color: lemon yellow with a slight fragrance of the ocean. Contentment. She would have no trouble accessing the power needed to be a protector.

Kendra went inside the hut for a few minutes, then rejoined me.

"Strength, and like you said, safety." She passed me on the way to the path. "Good. I don't need to worry about that."

Lunch at Sheena's was fun. Kendra couldn't quite cover her appreciation of the normal shifter beauty. We were visited by a handful of youngsters, under Sheena's watchful eye, and she had multiple invitations to various parties. She was safe with anyone on the island, and I didn't plan to lock her up. Teenagers needed fun as well as training.

HENRY ARRIVED MID-AFTERNOON. D told me to wait for them at The Inner Spell, promising to bring him up to us as soon as possible. I worried there was something wrong with Henry, that D didn't want me to meet him for a terrible reason.

"There is something wrong with him," Destroyer announced. "He is timid and that is not acceptable."

If Destroyer wasn't exaggerating, we would be in trouble. A protector needed to be open and willing to meet people.

I didn't pass on his words as Kendra and I waited at the entrance to the main building. I would have plenty of time to assess what Henry needed, and Kendra, because we were setting up residence here. Until I figured out when they could go out on their own.

Along with their rooms, I'd set up a chalet for each of them as a kind of private retreat and experiment lab when we got into spell work. It was much safer for everyone than the dining area or Mrs. V's cottage. Of course, I had no idea what spells we would be casting.

D stayed on the road and waved at me before cycling off. Henry parked his bike in the lot and grabbed his backpack off the parcel rack. He rushed over, a smile on his face. "Hello. I hope I'm not too late."

"Not at all," I said. "Come drop off your belongings and we'll get to know each other."

I'd brought in wine, beer, and the usual popular soft drinks. Kendra was too young to drink. Not that there was a law about it here, but she'd be going back to the mainland where there were all kinds of rules. I mean, I wouldn't be overindulging, but my nerves would benefit from a little loosening. I heard Henry's door open and close a couple of times before he finally joined us.

"I wasn't sure what to bring down with me," he said. "Decided that it was okay just to bring myself."

"Beer or wine?" Kendra asked. She'd appointed herself server for the evening. "Or tea?"

Henry's glance went between the three choices. It looked as if he was reading the items. A little gray confusion swirled through his aura. I knew one of his powers was predicting outcomes, but it seemed a bit over the top to use it to make simple choices. I tried not to make a judgment based on this short interaction, or at all, really.

"Beer please," he said. "Let me help. Are those Chips? And crackers. Lovely, best not to imbibe on an empty stomach."

He poured snacks into bowls and rejoined us at the table. The best thing about Henbane, as far as I was concerned, was the food and drink. Plenty of earth and kitchen witches in residence. Everything tasted like the ideal version of itself.

"I thought we should share a little about our lives so we get past the strangers phase."

I'd given a lot of thought to this, and talked with Mrs. V for hours. We needed them comfortable so they would learn from each other. Henry was so embedded in the plain human world, he'd have a completely different take on every aspect of our life. Kendra was young and brought a fresh perspective.

The truth is, I didn't want to be a teacher. This whole idea was about mentoring and critical thinking. Something I'd experienced with Mrs. V to widen my understanding of the magical world. It was worth the frequent bouts of frustration to figure things out for myself.

"You can follow me on our social media," Kendra said. "I'll send you the link. Send me yours, too. This is our spring break. I can stay for like a week or a bit more if I don't see my friends at all." She paused. "I am right? That I'm going back? This isn't going to be forever? The training, I mean. Like the protector thing is my life, but I get to finish school and say goodbye to my friends."

"It would be better for you to graduate," I said. "Taking you out of school is pretty complicated. You go to a plain human one?" She also needed a few years of experience, but

I remember how I felt at that age when people said I was too young to understand.

"Yeah. All of my friends are witches though. The plains hang out together but I guess they don't know we're witches."

Four more years shouldn't make a difference in the long run. Or maybe understanding plain humans more would make a positive difference. The main problem I could see is that she might be pulled away to save the world. Maybe there would be more protectors soon, or I could cover her until she was old enough. "That's the idea. You continue to go to school. Spend your vacations with us, or most of them."

She relaxed all over, as if her stress had been taking the place of her bones. "Good. What about you Mr. Curtis?"

"Please, it's Henry. I suppose my background is boring. I've been a librarian in Powell River for about twenty years. This protector power came at a good time because I needed to move on before people noticed I didn't age. My powers let me consider consequences, act as a mediator, and I can often make visible past actions. I don't find that as helpful as the others. I hope they will assist me in my new duties. I supposed I can be based here as long as people will have me. I could be elsewhere if that is required. I see no long term issue either way."

"We'll talk about that later, for now, why don't you both settle in. We're headed out to the bistro for dinner in a few hours." There was no reason for any of the icebreakers I'd devised. These two fit together as if they'd been close friends.

3

The next morning Mrs. V joined us for breakfast at Jan's. I'd learned a lot from trying to train protectors a few weeks ago and the biggest was not to isolate us at The Inner Spell. Yes, it was great to know where everyone was when it came to learning, but the killer had managed to set a stifling ward around us. This session we'd be talking to residents, gaining broad knowledge from Henbane. After that, Mrs. V suggested we go visit the other protectors. I wasn't crazy about traveling because Destroyer would be able to come with me. But whatever it took to get these two up and running was fine. And I wouldn't be able to stay on Henbane as a protector, anyway.

Jan served us himself, letting his staff take care of the other customers. I worked part-time for him when I first arrived. He did take breaks, but he was always here. His girlfriend ran the kitchen as if every meal or snack was being judged for a Micheline star.

"I can't keep eating like this," Henry said. "It's delicious and fuels my power, but I'll get fat."

Mrs. V gave him the side-eye. "Food is important. It's unusual for witches to gain weight. Why are you worried?"

He barked out a laugh. "I live with the plain humans. It's been a long time since I've been around other witches. I forgot about that. Plain humans who are the age I look, are always worried about extra weight. Once on, they can't seem to get it off."

"Why do you live like that?" Kendra asked. "Witches and shifters live with witches and shifters. Even in Vancouver we kept separate, even in school. Why would you choose to cut yourself off?"

It wasn't a bad question. I'd been told even solitaries who thought of plain humans as the biggest danger in the universe socialized with witches. I wasn't the only child I'd met who spent their lives as a plain, but in both circumstances, our powers were suppressed. If I'd known, I would have found others like me.

"My powers," Henry said. "Or rather one of them. Seeing the consequences of plain humans is like watching TV with the sound down. Easy to ignore. I think it's because I can't really help them. When I'm around magical people, it's like... well to use the same analogy, it's like having headphones on with the volume turned up all the way, and the speakers at the same time, but on a different channel."

"So you run away rather than figure out how to control it?" Kendra asked. Her tone was neutral, but I couldn't hear the words as anything but an accusation.

"Exactly," he said, apparently not taking offense. "It's easier to live with the guilt of abandoning people than to try to damp the volume."

Mrs. V waved for another pot of coffee. "You won't be a successful protector if we can't get you some control. Cossi, that's your lesson one for Henry. Now, Kendra, tell us a bit about you."

Kendra put her phone to the side. She'd been working hard to let it go, but I couldn't blame her. We needed to engage her, not punish her by cutting her off.

"I'm thirteen, so I guess there's not much. Like for me it's easier just to hang with my witch friends. I can tell when people are lying. It's kind of like a vibration in my teeth. Gross after a while, but I can handle it because we don't lie a lot. Plains, at least teenagers, lie all the time but I don't hang with them."

For the first time, I was grateful my parents suppressed my powers. What would my life be like if I saw emotions bleeding from everyone?

"So how do we know when we're protecting right?" Kendra asked. "Like is there a bunch of rules? Or a test?"

"No rules," Mrs. V answered before I could say anything. "Each situation is different. Or that's how it's been up to now. In my very long memory there never were."

"Perhaps some guidelines?" Henry said. "Surely after all the time we've lived alongside plain humans, there's enough data to build a... philosophy? Or some hind of matrix of suggested actions?"

"Tell them about your victories," Destroyer interrupted. "A long and successful carrier of defeating evil."

I rolled my eyes and noticed Mrs. V grin. Tulip must have passed on his words, or said something thuggish but similar. My experience was the most recent, so maybe Kendra would have an easier time relating to examples from her timeline.

"The familiars have a point," Mrs. V said, passing on the comments. "Stories are powerful tools."

Most of what I'd learned involved a murder, and that

wasn't really protector work. Except it did put us at risk of interference by plain human authorities. And maybe it was protector work, at least part of it.

I started with Marcus Reeves. "His power was so different the community didn't know how to manage him," I said. "We brought his family here where he could be safe while he learned control."

"I heard about him," Kendra said. "It's so cool he can bring art to life, right? It would be better if we lived openly. He would be a star."

"And how do you think a plain human would react?" Mrs. V asked.

"Yeah, haters. So it's not just shut down the problem, right?" Kendra looked into her empty coffee cup. "Can I have more?"

"Water or tea," Mrs. V said. "You are too young for that much coffee."

Jan brought a jug of water and glasses, and then left us to our discussion.

"It's about getting the outcome that protects us," I said. "I haven't encountered any situation yet that means we have to sacrifice a witch or shifter for the community. I think the right solution will always include solving the witch or shifter as well as the situation. If that makes sense."

The truth was that Phillip caused so much chaos that he'd sacrificed himself—I don't think it was a choice. The rebound of all those hexes had drained him of his magic and his life.

"And when you have to travel?" Henry asked. "What about your familiar? A crow is a challenge to take with you if it's international."

I heard a satisfied caw in the back of my mind. Destroyer disliked being forgotten. "Mine, yes. The only time I had to travel far away, he couldn't come, but he was helpful. You can speak to your familiar anywhere."

"In the old days, there were sufficient protectors that no one had to travel far," Mrs. V said. "I hope we are returning to that. It would only take three, maybe four, protectors to cover the Americas."

"Still too far to react fast, and take along a crow." My guess was we'd need a protector for every province and almost every state just to cover North America.

Kendra sighed. "I want a puppy. Or a kitten. If I get a familiar, I don't want to leave them behind."

Mrs. V had waited over a century to find Tulip. When Destroyer chose me, I wondered if having a familiar was part of being a protector, but she'd managed just fine without one. And in Germany, I was still able to talk to him. The time zones were a bit tricky, but we made it work.

My phone rang. I looked at the caller ID and asked Mrs. V, "Do you know an Alexi Babcock?"

"Raven's Rest, not far from here," Mrs. V said. "Answer it."

I didn't know where Raven's Rest was, like so much of the wider magical world. "Hello?"

The voice that answered buzzed with anxiety. A man by the depth of it. "Is this Cossi Fortuna?"

He called me, so that was a weird question. "Yes."

"We have a problem over here. I need a protector to convince someone they have gone too far."

4

Raven's Rest was a quiet subdivision outside Sechelt. One I'd never suspected existed so close to Henbane.

I made a mental note to think about creating a community listing. It would be longer than my mental list of to-dos and help us understand the connections between protectors and the people they were supposed to help. I added to my mental list a task to create a less unreliable one. Even if we couldn't get a worldwide one set up, I'd love to know the local ones, maybe including anything within a day's drive.

The article I found on a magic social media site told me that Sechelt wasn't that big. In the sixties, some witches got together to build a development just for magic users. The houses sold only to witches or shifters, and it was close enough to the schools and other services to be handy.

"This is a good opportunity to learn," I said. "We'll all go. It's close enough that Destroyer can join us."

"I am in flight as we speak," he announced. "Hurry before I solve this problem myself."

Mrs. V shook her head. "I will not leave Henbane. You

are quite capable of dealing with whatever the crisis turns out to be, if it's not being overblown."

"I meant Kendra and Henry," I said. "It's perfect for them to see how a protector works." Or at least, how I work.

"You need to get there soon," she said. "Even an overblown problem can be trouble so close to plain humans. Keep me updated."

With that, she left us. "I'll arrange for transport," I said. "Then we need to pack for a couple of days away."

"A field trip," Kendra said. "I'm in."

"Are you sure we should join you," Henry asked. "We could spend time studying while you are away. Having us there may complicate things."

Fieldwork was important. I couldn't manufacture scenarios well enough to get either of these two people ready fast enough. I mean, if the universe was creating more protectors, it might mean something bad was in the works. And what if more of them bloomed? How many could we take in? Then I remembered his power. How would he manage if he was inundated with visions of possible futures?

"Unless you have an vision of a bad outcome as a result of you both assisting, we'll all learn something," I said. Kendra's excitement didn't need any response.

"Until I know the problem, I cannot use my powers." He didn't sound happy about that. What must it be like to see all alternative futures? How does he ever make a decision?

"Then it's an chance to see how your powers help you protect," Kendra said. "Buck up. It will be fun."

Buck up? Did teenagers talk like that? I felt so old.

I was a lousy boat driver, so I sent a text to Mark asking if he'd take us over.

Thirty minutes on the wharf. Do I need to wait to bring you back?

I told him, probably not.

WHEN WE GOT to the dock after parking Beulah and the two community bikes in the lot, Mark was waiting in the boat. It was one of the shifter vessels. Sleek and fast.

"I've gathered a bunch of errands as usual," Mark said as he helped Kendra step onto the deck. "A couple in Vancouver. I'll check with you on the way back to see if you're ready to come home."

That gave us a few hours to resolve whatever problem made this Alexi guy call. If we hadn't solved the situation then, we'd at least know the extent of it.

"Can I learn to drive a boat?" Kendra asked. "Is there a legal age? Do I need a license?"

Mark pulled away from the dock. "We can teach you. But not on this one, too powerful. You need a license but we'll work that out."

The trip to Sechelt was short, maybe twenty minutes. I liked to watch Henbane retreat and then suddenly disappear. Okay, if I concentrated, I could still see a hint of it. The wards kept other boats away as if gentle currents warned of rocks. Not just for plain humans, even witches and shifters needed to be brought over the first time.

"Can we go shopping?" Kendra asked. "Before we go back. I mean obvs the problem is priority but... maybe I could get a bike like yours. And decorate it."

"There's not a lot of shopping here," Henry said. "Not malls like in Vancouver."

Kendra shrugged and followed me across the parking lot. The sound of Mark pulling away seemed to draw a line.

On this side, we were no longer residents of Henbane; we were on official business.

A tall man was walking toward us, not in a hurry but with purpose. He fit the description of Alexi Babcock: silver hair, neat beard. His clothes were meant for working outside, not in an office. Cargo pants, a collared tee, and hiking boots. All a dusty kind of brown.

I led my two students toward him. "Are you Alexi?"

"Yes, indeed. I know of you, Cossi Fortuna, but who are your companions?"

Before I could answer, Kendra stepped forward and held out her hand to shake. "Kendra Walsh. This is Henry Curtis. We're here to help out. New protectors."

Alexi's emotions flickered. Not just a new one coming in to replace the curiosity, but on and off like he had a malfunctioning shield. "I see. Well, good thing I brought the Jeep and not the Smart Car. I'm parked over there." He pointed at a dull green vehicle parked at the entrance to the lot. "We'll be in Raven's Rest shortly."

"They are waiting for you with the correct level of respect." Destroyer's voice in my head was comforting.

"What's the issue?" Kendra asked. "You didn't tell us anything on the phone. Is that normal?"

Alexi turned on to the main road and headed toward the hills. "All questions will be answered when we get there, if I can ask for a little more patience. This is something that our council will explain better."

I was pretty used to talking to councils. Every decent sized community had one. Their job was to make sure they witches and shifters were able to support themselves. And they kept an eye on the local threats. When I say I was used to it, all I had was Vancouver, *Sicherheim* in Germany, and I was a member of the Henbane one.

"How many council members do you have?" Henry asked. "Keeping you all safe must be a full time job."

"Five of us," Alexi said. "Me, Felix, Marina, Vijay, and Carmen. I'll introduce you to them when we arrive."

I turned to face Kendra and Henry. "I think we can let Alexi concentrate on the driving."

"Are you scared he'll get into an accident?" Kendra asked. "Like on Henbane you all ride bikes or walk. It's okay if you are a nervous passenger. Maybe Henry can see what's in the future so you can be calm."

That is not what I meant. But she was right. I wasn't a good passenger, and I didn't like to drive so that was a problem.

"I'd prefer to keep my thoughts in the present," Henry said. "No act is ever without risk."

Great. By his emotions, he meant the words to be reassuring.

"We're here," Alexi announced. "Take your bags; someone will take them to your rooms inside the Gathering House."

The building we stopped outside looked more like a First Nations long house than a community center. The odd thing was that it felt like The Inner Spell. A wide space that reminded me of a hotel lobby, with lots of seating. The wood posts were all well oiled and strong, the slate floor grounded the space and added to the feeling of welcome.

Four people stood in the lobby waiting for us. Alexi ushered us over to make the introductions. He gestured to each as he spoke their names. Carmen Oakes was short, iron gray haired, and smiling brightly. Vijay Sandhu looked like he was in his twenties, but I got an older vibe from him. Vibe? Was Kendra rubbing off on me? He was some kind of environmental scientist. Tall lean and with sparkling dark eyes, he shook our hands with a genuine smile.

Marina Seastorm was the tallest of them, her age looked to be around sixty, but you never knew with witches. She wore a lot of bangles and flowy clothes. Finally a neat man dressed nattily and almost bouncing on his toes with impatience, told us his name was Felix Park. Council meetings must be fun with Alexi and Felix being complete opposites.

"Come," Marina said. "Tea is ready and then we'll tell you everything. I said we should have done that when we called, but I was overruled."

5

The tea was an ordinary black blend. Nothing magical in it to help focus our minds. The cookies were home made; the flavor of lemon and black pepper danced on my tongue. The atmosphere of the small meeting room matched the refreshments, mostly functional but the tables and chairs were made of a light pine. The walls were a calming gray covered in art, everything from finger painting to intricate tapestries.

The emotions swirling around me did not match anything. Worry fizzed through the full range of feelings, a few spikes of fear and annoyance added a discordant prickle.

"Tell us what exactly prompted you to call," I said. I was tired of waiting for someone to speak and I had a creeping feeling this was going to be both dire and complicated. Perfect for training, but a bit like learning to swim by falling of a boat mid-ocean in a storm.

Carmen glanced around at her fellow council members and then took a deep breath. "I suppose I'm the best one to explain," she said. "I'm more neutral on this than others. Not that we are torn, just a bit conflicted."

I wanted to yell at her to stop stalling, but that wasn't the kind of reputation I intended to build. Or demonstrate for Henry and Kendra. "It's easier just to tell us. Until we know the details, we can't fix anything."

She nodded like I'd just made up her mind for her. "We have a resident who may be stepping into dangerous territory. Randi Fletcher. She's filming a documentary about our community. Planning to publish it, I suppose the best word is wide. The plain human social media as well as ours."

"We can probably tag that up as fake," Kendra said. "The plain humans will end up fighting about the latest conspiracy and no one credible will take any notice. It won't belong before something else takes their attention."

Henry looked at her appalled. "You can't guarantee that. In the future, someone might investigate it. Once anything is posted it's there forever. And, I see all of those consequence even before we ask questions."

It was far too soon to jump to solutions. Both of them were right in a way. I leaned more toward Henry's point. Protecting the community wasn't about fixing today's problem. We needed to fix it forever. "What exactly is this documentary about?"

Vijay took over the story. "Two thing of concern. The main thread is debunking myths about us. You can imagine what that would do to us. We'd have to leave everything and reestablish ourselves elsewhere. And we'd need notice that Randi won't give us. Our children would be uprooted. Perhaps we'd all end up in different places. The second is that she plans to highlight our garden. Where we've grown plants out of their habitat. We cannot allow her to expose us to scrutiny. People will come to see for themselves. We'll have to destroy it before someone ignored the wards"

"We'd be overrun with scientists doing field studies," Carmen added. "And tourists. And even locals. Our true nature would be exposed before we could escape even if she didn't go ahead with the documentary. Not only ours, but all communities eventually."

Yeah, that was the main problem. Kendra's plan might be okay for some story about witches living together, but actual plants growing in hostile environments. Carmen hadn't even mentioned the agribusinesses looking for new ways to increase yields. Or the GMO protests. Not only would it harm Raven's Rest, but Sechelt and possibly Henbane. I didn't know who much pressure any wards could take before failing.

"What kind of garden," I asked trying to stay in information gathering mode and not spinning off into panic. There was enough of that coming from the other witches in the room. Even Kendra was getting worried.

Excitement lightened Marina's worries. "I went to Henbane for the Summer Festival a few years ago. I know, it seems like we should be visiting all the time since it's just across the water, but life keeps us at home lot. I was so excited to see so many varieties of flora. It's partially my fault, I admit. Randi heard me rhapsodizing and suddenly we were agreeing to an Impossible Garden. I should have kept my thoughts to myself."

"Like a conservatory?" Kendra asked, ignoring—or not seeing—the fear. "Like at Little Mountain in Vancouver?"

"I've been there too and sort of," Marina said. "But our exotic plants aren't in a building."

"How did you allow this to happen?" Henry asked a little harshly.

I was happy to let them ask the obvious questions while I tried to think of a solution to the problem. We could talk about approach later. Not that this council had actually named the problem, just a bunch of possible outcomes that were scary enough.

"It's well hidden from view, the garden," Vijay said. "And to answer your question, we got caught up. When you meet Randi, you'll understand."

"So you have a garden that will raise suspicions, but that might be easily explained if anyone notices, and you have a witch who wants to publish a documentary?" I tried to push them along to the one thing we could deal with to prevent a future none of us wanted.

"Don't you think that's enough?" Alexi asked. "Should we have waited until the plain humans were overrunning our community?"

If not for my power I might have taken offense. The whole group radiated fear. That made people react badly and I could use it to get to the point.

"No. I want to make sure we have the whole story. Let's go look at the garden first. Then I want you to tell me what actions you've taken. Right now, we have nothing concrete to fix."

"Can't you just bind her with your magic?" Felix asked. "Stop her from endangering everyone?"

Kendra looked at me hopefully.

"You know her, and I'm sure you've tried that tactic, does she strike you as someone who will accept a limitation from a protector? Or will she try to find a loophole?"

"She will find a way to fool you into thinking she's stopping," Alexi said. "We have been here before on minor disagreements."

"Then you understand why bindings are a last resort." I

looked at Kendra when I said it. She needed to learn that lesson today. A teenager might not be able to think of the long-term repercussions.

THE GARDEN WAS WELL HIDDEN in the trees. Multiple look-away and go-somewhere-else charms ensured a hiker wouldn't stumble on it. Stronger wards were a good idea because these wouldn't stop someone who knew there was a garden to find.

What Marina described was a bit short of reality. Yes, the garden wasn't in a building engineered for different micro-climates. It was in a clearing where the trees had grown into a canopy which created warmth and shade where needed. Shafts of sunshine were directed to those plants needing light.

And the planting was done deliberately to integrate plants. Amongst the pineapples were delicate tropical orchids, an avocado tree heavy with fruit, a stand of tea bushes and banana palms grew opposite a cluster of coffee trees. The name fit; Impossible Garden. Before seeing it I'd thought maybe a few cacti or one of those savanna trees, acacia. Not the case.

This was like someone decided the restrictions of eating locally were too much and brought what they needed to change the definition of local.

The council was right about the threat. But we could reinforce the wards and monitor the area. This was too important to jump to clearing it out as a first step.

"Wow," Kendra said, "this is... wow."

Henry didn't speak. He was trembling. I reached out to take his hand.

“It’s okay,” I sent him some reassurance. “We’ll find a way to fix this.”

“Too many futures,” he whispered. “Good and bad, but mostly bad.”

The council members were clearly proud of their accomplishment. Along with that, they were afraid. Because I’d make them destroy it? Because they shouldn’t have agreed?

“What are you doing here?”

The voice preceded a woman slipping through the barrier of trees. Dressed like an old-fashioned photojournalist, cargo everything—all little pockets filled with supplies, and two cameras strung from straps around her neck.

6

"Randi," Alexi shouted and waved her over. "This is the protector, and her...colleagues. You should show them respect."

There was no way his words would fix the situation. I didn't want people respecting me because the universe picked me as a protector. I might be alone in that because Kendra stiffened beside me like she agreed with Alexi. Henry on the other hand was trying to look like he wasn't even here.

"That's fine," I said. "Perhaps we can talk at The Gathering House? Where we can have tea?"

"Where you can tell me to stop?" Randi asked. Her emotions told me exactly what she thought. Defiance swirled in a tight spiral of fuzzy orange.

"Where we can talk," I said. "I need all the facts, not just one side. And my colleagues are new protectors. Kendra and Henry need to learn how to get the full picture of any threat to the safety of our world."

I kept my voice soft as I spoke. If Randi thought I was going to upend her plans, she wouldn't cooperate. I wasn't all that sure she'd be helpful anyway, but all I could do was show I was open-minded.

Randi tapped several of her pockets while she thought. "Fine. Perhaps you can arrange for lunch, Carmen?"

"I'll call ahead," Carmen said.

I was really glad I didn't live here. Far from the supportive residents of Henbane, Raven's rest seemed to seethe with pettiness.

"I'll meet you there." Randi turned and reentered the cluster of trees.

LUNCH WAS DELIVERED AS SOON as Randi marched into the conference room. She'd taken time to change out of what I thought of as her field work outfit. Now she wore jeans and a green tee shirt with a jacket. The jacket had as many pockets as her earlier outfit. The cameras were gone, but she held her phone out and put it on the table. "I'm recording this. For the documentary. I won't film since you told me last time it was intrusive."

Kendra leaned in and whispered, "if she can't be nicer, no one will watch her documentary anyway."

"I heard that, young lady." Randi stared at Kendra as if she could freeze her in place. "Marketing my art is something I will need to research."

Okay. "Why don't you tell us about your projects while we eat," I said. "This looks delicious, Carmen. I'm impressed at how quickly you put together this barbecue lunch."

Three platters filled the center of the table. Each one piled high; ribs, corn, coleslaw. And a pile of hand wipes was set beside each seat.

Randi served herself and took a bit of everything before she spoke. "I don't know what the fuss is about."

"You are about to expose us," Alexi said. "With your plans. Your documentary will attract all kinds of plain humans to trample our lives. The garden cannot be explained without magic."

Randi waved a clean rib at him. "Pish. Why would the plain humans care. We're tucked away on The Sunshine Coast. I'm not inviting anyone. Just sharing the truth."

How much damage had that statement led to in the past. I saw Henry flinch. He was being inundated with possible outcomes. There must be a way to shield him somehow. This is just the kind of situation a protector faced. It was never black and white. And none of us wanted the magical world locked down. The garden seemed to be the way in. Something we could handle.

"Surely you see the risks," I said. "If even only the residents of Sechelt find out about the garden, how will you keep it safe?"

"There are wards. For the plain humans. Of course you were able to go there. Magical humans can find it, or be taken there. Plain humans will simply by misdirected. We are very good at hiding what we are. Not like Henbane. You have your wards and you daily life is not threatened by your neighbors."

Henry stopped pushing his food around the plate and said, "the wards only work because the plain human doesn't know there is anything worth finding. If they are purposefully looking for your Impossible Garden, they will eventually find it."

"Then we put up stronger wards," Randi announced.

This was going to be a long process. She had no intention of listening to anything we had to say. I couldn't just force her to change her mind with magic. That felt all kinds of wrong—at least for now. The protector power didn't rush to be used. That meant, other solutions were possible—or we haven't found the real danger yet.

"Why do you feel the need to publish your documentary on plain human platforms?" Kendra asked sounding far more mature than she was. Although I guess that might just be because she understood that world.

"The plain humans could gather some ideas about how to use the land without destroying it." Randi gestured with her fork as if the answer was obvious to anyone with a mind.

"They don't learn lessons," Kendra said. "They have lots of opportunity from other plain humans. And you could do that by setting up a fake profile and posting tips and other stuff. Why do you want to put us in danger? Are you just looking for attention?"

Wow. I waited for the reaction to unfold, waiting for the blow up.

"That's a good question," Alexi said, defusing the tension. "You can meet your goals in any number of other ways. Lots of witches sell products to plain humans without drawing attention to our world. Why must you risk everything?"

Randi didn't seem at all put out by Kendra's directness. Perhaps she appreciated it. Because she wasn't listening to any of the objections. She just waited for her turn to talk. "And how is that working out? I thought Raven's Rest needed income? This will solve our cash flow problems."

The other council members looked at each other. All I saw was surprise. Perhaps the community wasn't strapped for cash. Or perhaps it was surprise that Randi knew. Or that they had no idea if she was right or not.

"We are not rich," Vijay said wiping his hand on a napkin. "But we don't need money."

"Everyone needs money. Why don't we expand?" Randi

asked as she pushed her empty plate to the center. "We could start buying out our neighbors. Making Sechelt a haven for magical humans. Larger than Henbane."

I let them argue for a while. There was something missing. Not that Randi was lying, between us one of the protectors in the room would have noticed. Witches were humans and some of them would value money and status just like plain humans. But ignoring the danger was... stupid. I mean there was a slim chance that the plain humans would act differently from they way they usually did—kill anything that wasn't the same as them.

Being exposed seemed like it was a constant worry. Not like everyone was running around in a panic to stop it happening, but I guess like working in a bank. There was always a chance of a robbery, but you just go on with the job.

I glanced at Henry and Kendra. They were doing the same as I was, watching and listening. Of course, Kendra was leaning forward, ready to jump in if needed, and Henry was muttering to himself. I caught words that made me think he was tracking outcomes.

I grabbed my phone and sent a text to Mark. *We aren't coming home any time soon. Don't bother to come back here.*

He sent a thumbs up.

I stood, and all arguments stopped.

"I need to consult with my colleagues. We will meet again tomorrow. Randi, can we trust you not to do anything until I've had a chance to think about possible solutions?"

"I'm not ready yet anyway. Fine."

7

The Gathering House had a wing of guest rooms. Four in all, plenty for us since no one else was staying here. In the hall outside, I said to Kendra and Henry, "Settle in and we can meet in my room in thirty minutes?"

I needed to time to digest the events before I jumped into solving the problem. I knew Henry would appreciate some distance from the argument. Kendra almost vibrated with the desire to fix everything. I didn't plan on lecturing her on patience. I wasn't sure that we'd defined the problem yet. Trying to fix it would likely make it worse.

"Shall I find some tea?" Henry asked. "I'm sure there's a kitchen somewhere."

"I'll do it," Kendra said. "I can unpack later. I'm not hungry but does anyone want snacks?"

Nosing around finding supplies was probably a better way for her to burn off some energy than just waiting out the half hour. "No food for me," I said.

"I'm happy with tea," Henry said. He opened the door to

his room and slipped inside. The aura of overwhelm followed him.

Kendra tossed her backpack into her room and ran back to the public area. I hadn't meant to stand and watch them, but I was here in the hall assessing reactions.

I entered my own room and looked around.

"Open the window," Destroyer ordered. "An emperor is not to be kept waiting."

He was perched on a branch outside. I unlocked and slid the window open. He hopped on the sill and then into the room. "Adequate."

It was more than that. Not imperial quarters by any means, but there was a sitting area with a couch and coffee table, a small cafe table and two chairs. The TV faced the bed and there was plenty of closet space. I peeked into the bathroom, happy to see it had a bath as well as a separate shower and a long counter. Not that I had a lot of toiletries.

"Have you found out anything?" I asked.

"The local birds have heard of my army and are eager to join."

Great, imperial expansion wasn't what I needed. "Anything to help us solve this problem?" He knew exactly what I meant the first time.

"I have given orders to my new recruits. I anticipate a fast resolutions. Your students will gain great respect for you."

I rolled my eyes. "Okay. What about the ground animals? Is there a good place for me to find any?"

"That garden. The one you should dig up." He fluffed his feathers. "I will leave the decision to you even though a handful of my elite crows and eagles would destroy it in moments. It is not difficult for me to return to Henbane. I may have an eagle bring a few of the ground prey here as ambassadors."

That would be terrifying for them. To be carried here by a creature who thought of them as dinner. "No need. I'll go looking for agents tomorrow." It seemed to make him less argumentative if I used his terminology; agents, spies, whatever.

"Agreed." He turned and flew out the window.

I closed it. Raven's Rest might be a safe place, but too many plain humans lived close by. I wouldn't have left a ground-floor window open before I moved away from Vancouver so why start now?

I shook out the clothes I'd brought and put them in drawers. I put my bathroom stuff on the counter. I still had ten minutes before Kendra or Henry arrived. A good time to put everything down on paper. And to update Mrs. V.

"You have it in hand," she said after I told her the basics. "This Randi is delusional. You might want to bring in a healer to see if she is suffering from something that can be cured. Witches are less subject to plain human conditions, but it is possible. Regardless, I agree her plans are dangerous. It is possible they are not the main danger. How are your students?"

"One is burning to tell everyone what to do, the other is paralyzed by the number of options he sees. Is there something I can give Henry to help him?"

"Probably. You don't need help with Kendra?"

"She's young and she just needs to learn some skills. Henry should have a shield on his power so he could survive." Why didn't he? Perhaps living in the middle of the plain humans was enough.

"Talk to him," she said. "I don't want to advise you

without knowing what he's tried. Do you need anything else?"

"We're about to start talking through the situation," I said. "I'll send you a text later."

Kendra knocked on my door a minute after I hung up.

"I'm a bit early," she said. "Carmen gave me the tea. And some chocolates. She said they make their own. That garden is cool if we can have local chocolate. You know the usual stuff it's kind of bad for everyone involved, right?"

"Yes, but I guess it's chocolate so it gets a pass?" I'd never quite understood why the rules that applied to blood diamonds didn't apply chocolate. I guess there are some ethically sourced chocolate, so maybe I had it wrong.

"Yeah."

Kendra arranged the pot and mugs on the table. The box of chocolates went in the center. Good way to stop us eating them without thinking.

Henry came in and perched on the edge of the sofa. He wrapped his arms around his body like a hug. The imminent threat to our world could wait.

I asked him about shielding.

"I have a charm that used to work," he said. "It expired and I couldn't find another source. If this is how being a protector feels, I'm not sure how long I'll be able to stand it."

"Dude, what exactly do you feel," Kendra asked. She shifted to sit beside him and took his hand. "We'll find a way to help. But we need data. Just like this whole job. We need to understand the problem before fixing it."

Henry started explaining, and I was shocked. How was he still walking around and not curled up in a corner crying? His power was wrapping in him a cocoon of possible outcomes. He couldn't focus on the here and now.

"It's like I live in one of those pictures that look like nothing until you suddenly see a giraffe or something."

I took his other hand. "Let me in. I might be able to find the trigger." I'd never used my emotion power like this, but I had to try something.

"I can, maybe, do a protection. Like protecting you from your power. Not like shutting it down, but letting you turn it off if you need to, because I don't think you can just decide not to be a protector."

Henry nodded and held our hands tightly. I told Kendra to wait until I scanned him. A block like she described would be best, but it needed pinpoint accuracy.

In the center of Henry's emotions were three pools of color. I'd never scanned anyone this deeply. The pools must be his powers. I'd have to try it on Kendra before we acted to make sure I was reading this right.

"Kendra, can I scan you like this?" I asked. "I think I see the powers but I'm not sure."

She let go of Henry and took my other hand. "Is it going to feel weird?"

"I felt nothing," Henry said.

I went quickly to the same place in Kendra's emotions. Three pools of color. Her ability to read the truth a deep indigo, different from mine or Mark's—I already knew that. Her pattern recognition and light pink, and her boundaries power; a warm stone color, gray but also yellow and blue.

I told them what I saw.

"So I need to do something to block his power inside him." Kendra sat back letting go of our hands. "Never done it. But I can try. If Henry is okay with it."

"If we go in together, maybe you'll figure it out?" I didn't want him to suffer any longer than necessary, but the only way to help was bring Kendra with me. And there was no guarantee I'd understand what she proposed to do.

"How?" she asked. "I've never done that. Okay, I haven't done much so that's not a surprise. I mean I was just kind of a passenger before. This time I need to be there, like not just watching."

"Take my hand not Henry's." I said. To be honest, I was winging it but that seem a good start.

It turns out that being a protector must come with some extra mojo. I felt Kendra's power sitting on mine. I took her to the neon orange power. We couldn't talk and I was about to withdraw us to make a plan, when a net wrapped itself around the power. No, not a net, more like a caul. It was soft to look at and the power was still able to flow, but somehow muted.

"How's that?" Kendra asked as soon as we withdrew.

Henry already looked healthier. "So much better. What did you do?"

Kendra beamed in pride. "So, yeah. I just told my power to kind of soothe yours. It's going to keep working, but you can make it stop by thinking of it."

"How do I think of it, and will it go forever if I do that?"

Kendra was looking at her phone and typing into a search engine. "Here." She shoved a picture in front of us.

It was a lump of meat wrapped in exactly the same way as his power.

"And I just think of it?" Henry asked.

"Like think of it getting thinner or thicker depending on what you want. It should last forever and if you find a better way to control it, you can imagine it gone."

"For a child you are very wise," Henry said. "No let's figure out what we need to do."

8

Last night ended with us deciding we needed more information. It was clear Randi polarized people and didn't help herself by refusing to listen. She didn't seem to understand, or possibly care, that if she didn't hear other points of view, there would be no compromise and the result would not be in her favor.

My preference was that we'd solve the problem this morning and be back on Henbane for lunch. Experience told me we were just in the right place, it was only day two and the reality was more complex than it looked.

Breakfast was another delicious meal. I'm sure a kitchen witch was behind the food but it just seemed to show up. Bacon perfectly crispy, eggs runny for me and firm for the other two, pancakes, syrup and butter. Along with constant refills of the glorious coffee.

"Why can't we just put a restraint spell on her?" Kendra asked. "Isn't it illegal to disobey a protector? It should be."

"First, it's not about illegal or legal," I said after swallowing my mouthful of food. "Either something is forbidden or it's not. I don't remember seeing a line about being stubborn."

"There's a list?" she asked. "I could look at it for ways to stop her."

"You learned that when you were younger," Henry said. "Parents deliver it as a nursery rhyme usually. Unless things have changes since the dark ages when I was born."

"Ha ha. You aren't that old. Yeah, I remember, but it's like ten things."

"We'll talk about it when we get back on Henbane. Yes, it's a short list." I turned my attention to Henry. "How are you feeling this morning?"

He added sugar to his coffee and beamed at me. "Slept like a witch who hasn't slept well since his powers bloomed. No nightmares. I spent part of the morning testing this new ability. I call it volume control."

"I think you might be our secret weapon," I said.

WHEN WE WERE DONE EATING, Alexi joined us. He looked as if he'd been for a run before coming to the center. Witches didn't usually need to work at being fit, but I hear running has other benefits.

"I'm here to help," he said. "The other council members, too of course, but I'm the point person, if you will."

"I need to talk to some more people," Kendra said. "We need more views. How do I meet people?"

Still a bit too rushed, but she needed to find her own balance. And in our world, no one would take it wrong if a protector was brusque.

"I can arrange for someone to escort you," Alexi said. "You are splitting up?"

"We are," I said. "Henry is going into town to do a little

research, and maybe get a sense of what the plain humans think of Raven's Rest. I want to talk to Randi, one-on-one."

Alexi pulled out his phone and sent a series of texts. "My niece and nephew will come to escort Kendra. And Vijay will give you a ride into town, Henry. Just call him when you are ready to come back. Or there's a bus that stops just at the entrance."

My two students nodded and left us. I felt alone, which was weird since I'd always worked kind of alone. I mean, Mark and D were always helping, and Lilibeth, but they weren't protectors.

"Now, when you say you want to talk to Randi alone, are you sure?" Alexi was scrolling through messages as he talked. "I think she's out at the cliffs."

"You keep track of everyone?" That was incredibly intrusive. Although if everyone agreed, I suppose it was helpful. Did I imagine Randi would agree to being tagged? No.

"Like the find my friends thing?" He chuckled. "No. Can you imagine how confusing that would be? Randi mentioned trying to get a few establishing shots yesterday. I think that means for setting the scene? Like when a TV show flashes images of the city where they are set but not filmed in."

She sounded like a professional, but these days, it didn't take much more than a Google search to get the skills you need.

"Okay, so back to your question. Why wouldn't I want to be alone with her?" I didn't like these tiny peeks below the surface of the community. Was there some plan to stop her from telling me her side of the problem? Not just to announce and leave; to actually explain. I couldn't think of any reasoning she present that would reduce the danger.

Randi was working on the assumption that plain

humans would look away. She clearly hadn't been on their social media lately. Maybe she'd listen to me without the pressure of her peers. How could she not realize, posting something like her documentary would be like sugar to a two-year-old? Only one person needed to find it. One person with a following.

Alexi poured more coffee before he answered. "Nothing really, but she has a habit of heading into rather remote areas. Finding her might be a challenge. We wouldn't want you to get lost."

So I was being paranoid? Well, maybe but I didn't mind a hike.

"My familiar could guide me," I said. "Or any of the animals. You know I have that power. In fact, I need to head to the forest to ask for information."

Alexi's emotions flickered with frustration. "If something happens to you, how will your familiar tell us?"

"Doesn't anyone here have a familiar? He can reach out through that connection."

"None of us do," Alexi said. "You must know how rare familiars have become."

That was news to me. Maybe why Mrs. V didn't get one for so long. Maybe Tulip was a sign of the trend reversing. I just hoped the trend didn't mean any new ones would also be thugs.

"So I need a guide. Or can we call Randi to meet me at the garden?" I could chat with some of the creatures out there. One trip for two tasks.

"Ah somewhat neutral ground. Yes. I'll send her a text."

Randi didn't answer right away, and I didn't want to sit around waiting and trying not to suspect everything Alexi had to say. "I'll go for a walk around the neighborhood," I said and then headed into the lobby.

I was looking around the space. The reception desk was a slab of some dark wood on a stone block. Groups of chairs were clustered for chatting, a coffee and tea stand. A bookshelf, a pile of board games. A community space that looked well used.

The doors stood open, I hoped they were closed at night or at least heavily warded. Today, the only living creature in sight was a puppy sniffing around the chairs. It was one of those teddy bear dogs, a Samoyed, I think.

"Hi, are you looking for your human?" I asked. No one had a familiar, so this must be a pet.

"Are you her?" he asked. His voice like a five-year-old.

"I don't think so," I said. Destroyer cawed in offense. I guess witches with emperor familiars didn't get pets. Even cuddly ones like this puppy. "What's your name?"

"Pickle. She was here. I'll come back."

He trotted out of the building without looking back. He's going to be fine, I told myself. He's well groomed and healthy. He'll be just fine this is not a plain human neighborhood. No witch would hurt him.

Alexi joined me in the lobby after Pickle left. He held out his phone. "I have confirmation that Randi is at the cliffs. Shall we go?"

I was dressed for a hike, so I might as well go now. Before I could tell him, a car slammed on its brakes outside. A man rushed toward us, his jacket flowing behind him, as if he was fighting a strong wind.

"Quinn, slow down, man," Alexi said, taking a step forward.

"No. Something very bad happened," he gasped for breath. "Randi. She fell. At the cliffs. Hikers saw her body, plain human ones. The police are on their way. This is a disaster."

9

"Quinn is Randi's house mate. He's married to Isabel," Alexi said. "I suppose longer introductions will need to wait."

I sent a text to Kendra and Henry. I wasn't calling them back from their tasks, just letting them know.

"Take me there," I said as soon as I put the phone away. "I need to see everything."

"But the plain humans," Quinn said. "Randi's death has made us vulnerable."

I took a breath, reminding myself that his words only came across as harsh because he was afraid. And panicked. I got it, having Randi's death under investigation by plain human cops was a potential disaster. But Raven's Rest must have plans anticipating something like this happening. Living almost elbow to elbow with the plain humans meant the community had more contact than most. The council would have created all kinds of contingency plans.

"We can deal with that easily," I said. "Where were you when it happened?"

"I had nothing to do with it," Quinn snapped out the words.

"I'm sure the protector didn't mean you did anything wrong," Alexi said. "You may have seen something. Why don't I drive us close to the area and then we can see what needs to be done, if anything."

"Oh, of course," Quinn said. "Forgive me, protector, you don't know me but I'm one of her few friends. I was there looking for her. I got worried she hadn't come back. I saw the commotion and then her body."

We piled in to Alexi's Jeep. Quinn in the back seat. "We should go to where she feel from," I said. "We should be able to see the body and the plain humans from there."

I was hoping we could find something to redirect the police attention. I needed them to decide it wasn't suspicious so that I could investigate with Kendra and Henry. The most worrying part was I still felt danger. Possibly because of the plain human police. I could only hope that was the case.

"We'll have to hike for a while," Alexi said. "It's not difficult, but we'll start at the parking lot."

"That's where all the plain humans are," Quinn said. "They will stop us. Interrogate us, take our DNA."

His over dramatic reaction was getting on my nerves. "We can use some look away charms. Just until we're out of sight."

"Do you have them. Is that something protectors do? Like always being prepared?"

I glanced at him in the rear-view mirror. Alexi was concentrating on the drive and no help in calming Quinn.

"We're not like the scouts," I said. "And I don't know about the others, but I like to keep charms I might need."

"It will be okay, Quinn," Alexi finally said. "We have three protectors here."

"I am arriving at the site," Destroyer announced.

"Where she fell from?" I asked aloud. "Sorry, I'm talking to my familiar." I added when both Alexi and Quinn looked puzzled.

"Yes. The body remains at the bottom. The plain humans are inspecting it. I do not think she will be moved soon."

"Can you see anything that might explain why she fell?"

He gave me that little caw I'd learned was his equivalent of a sigh.

"Okay, right. You don't know what that might be." I thought for a while about how to explain it. "Scuffed ground, blood?"

"None. The plain humans are coming up to see this place," he said.

"Don't do anything a imperial," I said. "Act like a regular crow."

"I am aware of the need to stay incognito." He went silent.

"The cops are looking for evidence at the top of the trail," I said. "We can't go up now, but my familiar is watching."

"Should we still go?" Quinn asked. "Perhaps we should wait?"

"For how long?" Alexi asked. "We don't know when the police will finish. We need to gather information to report to the council."

"Of course we still go," I said. "Quinn, don't mention that you found her if anyone asks."

"I think the hikers may have seen me," he said. "I didn't go near them, but I didn't hide. I was in shock."

Complication.

"Don't volunteer, but don't lie if you're asked. We're from her community, we heard there was an accident. We came to check. If needed we identify her. But nothing about her filming a documentary, or the garden."

"Yes, that will be best," Alexi said. Relief flowed from him as if he'd been worried I wouldn't have a plan. "Quinn can you manage?"

"I don't know. Perhaps you should leave me out of it."

I weighed the decision. In all it would be better to drop him off before we got to the site.

"I can leave you near the gas station," Alexi said echoing my thoughts. "You should wait there until we return."

Another wave of relief hit me.

"I won't move. I promise."

Two minutes later we dropped him at a small path about a hundred yards from the gas station.

"I suppose we park and wait," Alexi said. He didn't pull out onto the road. "We won't be welcome at the top."

"Let me see if my familiar has any information before we decide."

"Destroyer, what's happening?"

"The plain humans looked around and pointed at several places. The rocks were wet. Then they left. I do not speak human so I do not know what they said."

I passed that to Alexi. "Is it suspicious that the path was partially wet?"

"There are a number of streams that exit the rock face, so perhaps not."

I turned my attention back to Destroyer. "If I say some words, will you know if the police said them?"

"I am the emperor. This lack of knowledge is an oversight I will address immediately. Learning human should be easy for even a stupid crow, which I am not. Humans speak it after all."

I had no doubt he'd learn to understand English. "That didn't answer my question."

"Try and we shall see."

I couldn't do any harm by suggesting what I hoped was the outcome. "Accident? Unfortunate?" Then to be thorough, "suspicious? murder?"

"Yes."

He was determined to be a pain. "Are you mad that I liked the puppy?"

"You have no reason to want another animal," he said. "You have a perfect familiar."

"True. So, which words?"

He cawed smugly. "Accident."

I rolled down the window and called Quinn to get back in the Jeep. "We can go back to the Gathering House and wait for the police to inform us."

Alexi checked the road and pulled a u-turn heading back the way we'd come.

I sent a text to get Kendra and Henry back so I could update them.

Time to start figuring out our next steps. "Quinn, would Kendra have ID on her?"

"Yes. She always carried her driver's license, even though she didn't have a car. She liked the idea of having it. She said if someone asked her to join some group as an expert, they would need to know who she was."

I guess it was better to get the police part over with. "They'll go to her address. Is your wife there?"

"Yes, but she doesn't know." Quinn's panic spiked again. "Should I tell her? Should we go there?"

I needed all the time I could get to calm him down and

stop him from blabbing details that might make the cops suspicious.

"Tell her to come to the Gathering House, and let her neighbors know so they can send the cops to us."

10

Kendra and Henry were both waiting for me when we arrived. Isabel made it only ten minutes before the cops showed up. Alexi joined Quinn and Isabel as their adviser. Since he stepped into that role, I wasn't allowed in the interview. It all felt like I was watching a video in double speed. I wanted to be there, and I didn't have time to drop a listening charm.

The only option left was to talk about our next steps. I chose to stay in the lobby rather than go back to our rooms. Here, we'd see the cops leave and I could read their emotions. Knowing if they were still questioning the cause would go a long way to helping us mitigate the damage.

"So what are we going to do?" Kendra asked. "I mean with the cops. Obviously we'll find out who killed her. Like this wasn't really an accident, right?"

At least I could answer this question with confidence. "We're lucky because it looks like an accident. Alexi will do what he can to get the police to believe it. Unless there's some physical evidence, we should be okay. I don't know if it's murder, but until we have proof otherwise, this is a murder."

"What kind of evidence?" Henry asked. "My power is sorting through outcomes. It's odd to see that happen without being knocked into a panic. Thank you, Kendra, for freeing me from the daily battle with my power. But there isn't enough data to settle on a few options. And I can't just ask if this was murder and who did it because that's not a consequence. I will certainly explore new aspects no I have control."

"DNA, right?" Kendra said. "Like under her fingernails if she fought back. Or a hair caught in her clothes?"

We didn't want it to get that far. "Yes. I don't know about an autopsy. Would they push for one if we do a good job of making them think it's an accident?"

Kendra started typing on her phone. "Got it. It's kind of a maybe. If the coroner doesn't think there's foul play, they can waive the autopsy. The next of kin have something to say about it. I wonder who that is."

Alexi would know. I hoped he wouldn't try magic to persuade the police because that could backfire. He could convince them to save the expenses.

"We'll ask." I made a note to get Randi's background before we started our investigation. "It doesn't really matter that much what the plain humans think as long as they stay out of our way. Remember, far as we're concerned this is murder unless we prove otherwise. We know that her actions would have exposed more than a few secrets. The plain cops wouldn't see it as a motive."

"And no one will tell them," Henry said. "Not about the garden, or the documentary. The reason we were called here has been resolved."

"I didn't even thing of that," Kendra said. "So do we need

the community to ask us to solve her death? Like we can't just take it over?"

"It's a threat to our world," I said. "If she'd been found by a witch, we wouldn't be involved. But plain humans are curious. They need a reason to forget, and you both know we can't manipulate their memories. To protect the magical world, we need an acceptable conclusion for the plain humans." I held back my creeping feeling that the danger was still very present.

"It would be better if we knew what was going on in that interview," Kendra said. "If Alexi hadn't barged in, you or Henry could have been the adviser."

At least she knew a thirteen-year-old wasn't a good choice. "Alexi knows the two witches, and Randi. He'll be more effective than I would. But yeah, I should have thought to have my familiar listen in."

"I am marshaling my forces," Destroyer announced. "I would have sent a ground animal had I known."

"Things are moving too fast," I said to him in my mind. "We'll take control soon."

"Our plan?" Henry asked. "You have experience in murders. Where do we start?"

The only thing my previous investigations taught me was you dug out information until something connected. "We need a list of suspects and motives," I said. "And not a list of all the residents, it needs to be narrower. We follow up on what people tell us. We eventually find the truth."

"We can make people tell us the truth," Kendra said. "We're protectors. If we think people are lying, we use our power."

Henry saved me from explaining. "People lie about all kinds of things, Kendra. Mostly not about killing someone.

And I am not comfortable using my power to force secrets. I'm not sure that will even work."

Voices came from the hall leading to the conference room. Alexi and two others.

"Can we expect to hold our funeral soon?" Alexi asked. "The whole community is saddened by Randi's death."

"I need to talk to the coroner," a male voice answered. They stepped into view as he continued. "It's not up to us, but it looks like an accident. We're always worried about people hiking alone. I'll get back to her friends as soon as I can. You're sure there's no other relatives?"

"She had no family," Alexi said.

"Shouldn't be more than a couple of days," the female cop said. "No backlog right now."

Alexi ushered the police out and stood watching until they drove away.

"It went well," he said. "You'll want to talk to Quinn and Isabel now?"

"If they are ready," I said. Not that I was going to delay long, but we could give them a short time to collect themselves if needed.

"Better to get it over with, I think," Alexi said. "Then they can go home and start healing."

We were sitting around the conference table withing minutes. Both Isabel and Quinn refused refreshments. Their auras flood with sadness. Randi might have been a pain to the council and a threat to the whole magical world, but these two witches loved her.

Kendra placed her phone on the table to record. Henry sat back to listen.

"Did she have a next of kin? Or were you telling the truth?" I asked.

"Me." Quinn held up his hand as if he needed to catch

our attention. "Not related, but she listed me as her next of kin on all official documents. It seemed to be acceptable to the detectives."

I refused to feel more than a little happy with that even though I wanted to celebrate. Until the police told Quinn it was ruled an accident, we were still at risk of having to work around an official investigation.

"What did the police want to know?" I asked. We needed a place to start, and I hoped that something important slipped out. I'd call Mark later for advice but this was our case to solve.

"Why she was up there alone," Isabel said. "I told them that she went the all the time. That she was trying to capture a few more pictures for her publication."

"We didn't think it was a good idea to talk about the documentary," Quinn said. "I said it was a photography book."

Harmless enough, and I couldn't sense any lies. "Did they tell you anything about what the think?"

"Like they said," Alexi answered, "it looks like an accident. I wish we had her camera. They took it from her body."

"Will we get it back?" Isabel asked. "She had a lot of pictures on it. She wouldn't upload to the cloud."

"I believe if they rule it an accident, you will receive her belongings," Henry said. "I had a lot of time to study at my last job."

"What do you think?" I asked. "Is she likely to have fallen?"

Quinn flashed anger at me before he gained control. "She was like a mountain goat. If she fell, there will be something. A heart attack or a stroke. Otherwise Randi would still be with us."

"What about a struggle," Kendra asked. "Like maybe it was an accident because she was fighting with someone."

"Or, someone murdered her," Quinn said. "If you want the truth, I think someone pushed her. I think the motive is something she found in gathering stories for her documentary. Or just the fact she was going to publish."

Isabel nodded in agreement. "She was passionate and some people took it the wrong way."

"Then we investigate it as a murder," I said. "If the police ask you more questions, do you think you can convince them it was an accident?"

"Of course," Alexi said. "We're used to presenting an alternate version to plain humans. I did my best to nudge them along."

I couldn't help thinking that camera was a problem. There was nothing I could do about it until we knew.

"We need a list of people you suspect," I said. "Something to get us started."

Alexi dug out paper and a couple of pens from the credenza.

11

A half hour later, we were back in my room trying to make sense of the information Isabel and Quinn gave us. The list of possible suspects was way too long. Beside each name was a motive. Mostly just that Randi had annoyed someone too much.

"Is annoying a strong motive?" Kendra asked. "I mean if it is why aren't half the people on earth dead and the other half in prison?"

Her emotions and tone told me she meant it as a joke, but I thought it was a strong question. "Anything is a motive for the right person," I said. "But I don't think it is in this case. We're going to interview all the names on the list just in case. What Isabel and Quinn think is an annoyance, could be something more serious."

Henry held out the sheet of paper covered in columns. "This might be every adult in Raven's Rest."

"It will take forever," Kendra said.

"Let's figure out an order," I said. "Start with the most likely suspects and we might find what we need in the top ten."

“Excellent idea, empress protector,” Destroyer announced. “I have reports.”

I told Henry and Kendra we had some names from the animals at the site. “Destroyer is relaying it so, you add them to the list, or put a star or something next to the name.”

“You are fortunate that I was able to gather identities,” Destroyer said. “I have four witches that were near the site of the murder that day.”

I was usually stuck trying to dig out enough details to translate from what a squirrel thought was important so I could tie a witch to the clues. Mostly, animals started with just a witch and a he or she. A few times, they were able to say tall or short.

“Go ahead,” I said.

“I have two eagles and a wolf,” Destroyer said. “They each heard a name as the witches spoke to each other. They were spying on my orders. Jorge is the name said by the pair of witches who passed him coming from the top of the trail. Maggie and James. They greeted each other.”

It should be easy enough to get last names to fill in the data. “And the fourth?”

“Your guide. Alexi. The wolf followed him down the trail before the Jorge witch arrived.”

I stifled my reaction. At least I tried, but Destroyer ignored shields and Henry and Kendra were protectors. I wasn’t sure how successful I was. I remembered Alexi showing up sweaty and a little out of breath, like he’d been on a run—or a hike.

“Did any of your agents see what happened?” I asked. “Or see Randi?”

“A sparrow said she was there for a long time taking pictures. A long time for a sparrow could be only one minute.”

"Thanks," I said to him. "Let me know if you learn anything more."

"The puppy," he said, surprising me. "Watch for him." Then he cut off our connection.

What the heck? Was the puppy a possible killer? A spy? I reached out for an explanation, but Destroyer ignored me.

"Alexi?" Kendra said. "He didn't mention he was there."

"Don't make assumptions," Henry said. "Remember he was in shock over losing Randi, and then had to deal with the police. Perhaps he simply didn't have time."

Or he knew that none of us would be able to detect a lie if he simple didn't speak. But he'd brought us here to solve the danger, and his emotions seemed genuine.

"Let's look up the people," I said to change the subject. "Jorge? Is that name on the list?"

Henry ran his finger down the columns. "Jorge Rodriguez. One of the many names with annoying written beside it."

"Maggie Bell," Kendra said reading over Henry's shoulder. "Solitary. Something about a fight with Randi over bringing unwanted attention. And here's James Brightwater, Randi filmed his studio without permission and refused to delete it."

"What does it say Alexi's motive is?"

"Annoying again," Kendra said. "It's probably more than that, right? He was genuinely scared when he called."

"Yes."

"How do you plan to sort the list?" Henry asked. "I could use my power to see some ramifications, but that won't tell us who. I mean my question would be what could happen if the killer is and name someone. But we would be doing it for hours, and not get our answer. Unless you have a better suggestion."

"Too bad none of us can just ask our protector power," Kendra said.

That would be far too easy, and she was right. Why was this job so hard?

"If everyone is on the list, maybe we start with the council," Henry said. "Interviewing them will give us more information on the other names. And they have a broader perspective."

"You don't think a councilor is a killer?" Kendra asked. "They take an oath. What about the four from Destroyer?"

It was probably the wrong time to explain how Phillip avoided the oath. "Councilors first, is a good plan," I said. "Alexi is the only witch on both lists. We start with the council. Alexi last so we have crossover into the non-official witches. As for the rest of the list, is there a motive that might be more useful than the others?"

"One," Henry said. "Theresa Kimura. She works at the library. I can interview her since we have that background in common. It says she worked with Randi early on and was the first to point out the dangers."

So, nine suspects. Or rather nine of a long list who might actually be suspects.

"I think we should stay together on the interviews," I said. "It will save time, and three heads are way better than one. So, Henry, we'll bring Theresa here and you lead the questioning. If she's not a suspect we go to the council members."

"Thank goodness," Kendra said. "I wasn't looking forward to doing solo stuff."

We spent the evening planning our approach and sending interview times to the people on the list. Carmen told us she'd reserved the conference room for our investigation.

"If she's so helpful, how can she be guilty?" Kendra asked.

"She may think it puts us off track," Henry said. "I think you would benefit from a reading list of excellent detective novels. They tell you a lot about human behavior. And in this case witches are the same as the plain ones. I will text you links."

I expected her to roll her eyes and say something about old technology, but Kendra shone with excitement. "That's the kind of studying I like."

"Before we head off to sleep, I have two questions," I said. "Do you need a sleep tea?"

Kendra shook her head.

"I will make a pot, would you like me to drop off a cup?" Henry asked.

"Please. I need to be fully alert tomorrow."

"What's the other question?" Kendra asked.

"Have either of you seen a white puppy around? Destroyer said to watch out for him."

Neither of my apprentices had seen the little cutie.

"Is he rabid?" Henry asked.

"Not when I saw him," I said. He seemed completely healthy.

"What did your familiar actually say?" Henry asked.

"To watch for him."

"So not to watch out for him," Kendra said. "Maybe he saw something. And he can tell us who killed Randi?"

I would ask Destroyer what he meant when I talked to him later. I didn't want the puppy to be the problem here. I couldn't see him getting to the top of the path, let alone pushing Randi off.

12

The next morning Theresa Kimura presented herself at the conference room at nine the next morning. Since we'd be doing multiple interviews, we'd rearranged the chairs. Our interviewee would sit facing the door on the only seat that side of the table. Our chairs were set facing the hot seat, and spread out a bit. The rest of the chairs were stored in the empty room next door. The setup meant our suspect couldn't run out of the room if they turned out to be guilty.

"Theresa, what can you tell me about Randi?" Henry asked. He'd locked down his power to help him concentrate on the questions. He was learning how to manage the new ability to damp down the power fast. "Why would anyone try to kill her."

She sat bolt upright. "Well, they didn't try, did they? Are you saying this was murder? The plain humans think it's an accident."

"We hope that they will continue to think that," Henry said. "We also think that it might not be so simple. How did you hear what the plain humans think?"

"They are talking about it. In the library. Not all of them, but the usual gossips. I think one of the women was married to the detective. They think we're weird hippies in Raven's Rest. Said the trail should be made safer. That hikers need to be protected. Sad for Randi. But mostly concerned for themselves, as usual."

I liked her straightforward attitude. I imagined her standing at the checkout desk, listening in on all the chatting. Silently judging the gossips as they judged everyone.

"That is good information," Henry said. "If the plain humans put up fences or guardrails, would that have an impact on Raven's Rest?"

"You mean enough to bring in a protector?" Theresa waited for his nod before continuing. "No. It's not on our land. Not even close. That garden is well hidden and is in our control. I might even agree about the trail. Although, it's not exactly class 4, is it?"

"I'm not familiar with the different rankings of hiking," Henry said.

Kendra was typing notes into her phone while it recorded. I concentrated on reading Theresa. Nothing concerning in her aura, just a little impatience.

"Highest effort. More like beginner climbing. Sometimes need a rope. I can recommend some books."

"Thank you. I look forward to reading them. Now. Back to my question. Why would someone kill Randi?"

Theresa thought about the answer. I appreciated the effort. The last thing we needed was 'because she was annoying' as a motive.

"Look, she was always a pain. She'd get her head set on an idea and no one could talk her out of following it. Has been even when she was a kid. I remember she wanted to build a kid's play area close to the entrance to Raven's Rest.

The council at the time said it would be too risky. Plain humans would want to use it." She took a breath. "So she built it over night, thinking people would be happy when it was there—asking forgiveness not permission, that sort of nonsense. The council dismantled and rebuilt it closer to the forest. She got what she wanted, but no one understood why she had to pick the most dangerous place instead of just putting it deeper in."

"So you think this documentary is the latest example?" Henry asked. "Of her not understanding the wider issues?"

"It gets tiring dealing with someone like Randi. Someone who likes doing things the hard way. This time no one could figure out a solution."

I glanced at Kendra because I could feel her struggle not to interrupt. I shook my head. We would do the second round soon, but now Henry was in control of leading Theresa down our path.

"Is there anything we should know?" Henry asked.

It was a much broader question than I expected.

"She had a falling out with Alexi a few months ago. To be honest, I thought at the time she was losing it. He didn't do anything to make her angry. This whole situation makes me think she needed some healing. But she wouldn't hear of it." She rubbed her forehead. "If only she listened."

"Thank you," Henry said. "If you would wait here for a few minutes, I'll confer with my colleagues."

In the hall outside, Henry dropped a charm to keep anyone hearing what we said. "Well? I think we know she isn't the killer."

"You could ask her," Kendra said. "Right out. If she killed her. We'll know if she's lying, right? And ask her if she knows who might have killed Randi."

"If we ask that question first, our subject may get defensive," Henry said. "We know two new things. Randi was always annoying. And she fought with Alexi. Oh, and a third. She may have been mentally unstable."

"Why wouldn't we get that information after we asked the real questions?" Kendra was a bundle of confusion.

"Theresa might have become offended," I said. "In that case, she might not have thought we needed the background. Or maybe knowing we believed her, she might not have thought about why or who."

"Okay, so we ask now?" Kendra said practically bouncing with impatience.

"Yes," Henry said. "Unless there are other questions."

"I have one," I said. "We should ask who she thinks should be our number one suspect. It's a bit different from asking who she thinks might have done it."

It took less than five minutes to get our answers. Not the killer, and no idea who would have killed her. Our third question made her think. I wanted Henry to ask it because she might not know who did it, but knowing who was most likely was a competently different thing.

"I'm not saying they are killers, but you might look very closely at the council members. Randi was a much bigger problem for them. I guess that's why they called you."

We escorted Theresa to the lobby and watched her drive off to work. Our next interview was Vijay Sandhu. And he was due soon.

"I'll lead the next interview," I said. "Then Kendra, if you feel up to it."

"They won't answer my questions," she said. "I'm thirteen."

"You are a protector," Henry said before I could answer. "Your age means you need some life lessons, but do not let anyone treat you like a child."

Kendra straightened her back. If I'd said that to her, I would be worried she'd feel reprimanded, but Henry was her peer. So was I but I'm not sure she believed that yet.

"I'll watch you and learn. If I get it wrong, you can step in." There was that surprise maturity again. I knew witches of a hundred and ten who wouldn't think they needed to learn.

"We will have your back," I said. "If you need us to step in, tell us don't wait."

"Shall I make more tea?" Henry asked.

He turned to the kettle on the small refreshment stand when we said yes. I looked through the doors hoping to see Vijay. Instead, I saw the puppy. He was walking past and turned to glance in. Then he jumped in place and raced to the door.

Thank goodness it was open because he might have broken his neck trying to burst through.

"My witch," I heard in my mind as he jumped up and yipped at Kendra.

"My familiar?" Kendra asked me.

"Did you hear him speak?"

"Yes."

"Then he's yours. We'll ask Vijay if he knows where he comes from. And we'll need to get some food for him."

She wasn't really listening to me. Pickle was in her arms and licking her face.

"Kendra?" I said to get her attention.

"Yes?" Her eyes were shining and joy was the only emotion I could read.

"Do you want to continue the investigation?"

"Sorry," she said putting Pickle on the floor. "Yes. Pickle can be quiet and sit in the corner."

I very much doubted a puppy would be able to sit still

for long before the zoomies took over. But I wasn't getting between a witch and her familiar.

13

We only had a few minutes before Vijay followed us into the conference room. I sat back waiting for Kendra to get ready. Pickle sat under the table, leaning against her leg. Should I feel jealous that her familiar was cuddly and adoring? No. I had the best familiar in the world. An imperial crow with brains and a spy network. I didn't need cuddles and adoration.

"Thanks for coming," Kendra said as she laid out a pad and pencil on the table. Her phone followed. "I'll record the session so that we can listen later. It means you won't have to come back so much."

I liked that she didn't ask permission. I mean I sometimes did, but for a thirteen-year-old, it was good to sound confident. I was the only one who knew she was not. Her aura shivered with green anxiety. But she was covering it well and Vijay's powers didn't cover any emotional reading.

"I'm here to help as best I can," Vijay said. "This is awful. I mean Randi was a problem, but to kill her?"

"It is extreme," Kendra said. "We're asking everyone the

same questions, more or less. Let's start with where you were this morning."

"On the coast. I monitor and report to the Parks Canada for any environmental or weather related issues." He sat back satisfied with his answer and feeling a little pride in his important job.

She didn't react to his feelings. "Can anyone confirm your alibi?"

"Alibi? I can't be a suspect. I'm a council member." Now he was hurt, offended, and shocked. Good.

Kendra just waited.

He hurried to fill the silence. "No one in the area, but if you must find someone, I was on the radio with my contact so it will be a plain human. Do you want the information?"

"Maybe later," Kendra made a note on the pad.

"Am I truly a suspect?" Vijay's emotions changed again to curiosity. I'd never met a witch before who could toss emotions aside like they were looking for a nice outfit in their closet.

"Right now, yes. Everyone in Raven's Rest is. Until we have more information, we can't eliminate anyone." Kendra checked that her phone was recording. "I suppose we can get to the point. Did you kill Randi?"

"No. I would never take a life." He folded his arms on the table. "Are you satisfied?"

He wasn't being as aggressive as his words seemed. His aura still showed more curiosity than upset. And he didn't lie when he answered her question. I mentally crossed him off the list.

"Who do you think might be the killer?" Kendra asked.

"Are you sure it is murder?"

"We think so."

I felt Henry tighten beside me. Maybe he had doubts.

Another mental note to check later and a second to get a notebook and stop keeping so many tasks in my head.

"Then I would say no one in Raven's Rest is a killer. But since the facts point to someone here. Is it possible a plain human killed her?"

We hadn't considered that possibility. I was sure we were looking for a witch. I mean, my power was sure.

"Would one have motive?" Kendra's anxiety was gone.

"She barely interacted with us let alone the larger community," Vijay said. "No. If there is a killer, it must be a witch."

Kendra waited again. I liked the way the two protectors approached the interviews differently. And I would have a separate approach. In the past, I dug around pretty randomly for information.

"Oh, well," Vijay continued when it was obvious Kendra wouldn't speak. "Perhaps someone close to her. Isabel or Quinn? No. I can't see that. She had a falling out with Alexi, but he wouldn't take such drastic action. One of the other council members? Perhaps Marina? Well, I don't like to say."

I hoped one of the people on our list had more information than this. Or an ability to see their neighbors as something more than angels.

"I'm sure whoever did this, it wasn't purposeful," he said to himself. "The idea of her bringing the attention of the plain world is quite frightening. And frightened people do act out of character."

"True," Kendra said.

"You know," Vijay continued on a roll now his name was cleared. "Did you confirm her plans were such a danger? I mean, we all agreed it was, but isn't there some protector spell or ritual that allows you to confirm it?"

His was the first question like that and I was embarrassed that I hadn't thought of it.

Kendra turned to me. "Since I'm new to this role, I'll ask Cossi to fill us all in."

"As protectors, we know it was dangerous," I said. "But you may be right. It isn't easy for some people to trust a feeling." My mind was crawling through my memories of training. Nothing came to mind.

He straightened and looked at me, ignoring Henry and Kendra. "Perhaps this murder happened because the killer was unsure of your commitment. I'm not blaming you, just opening up some new thoughts."

That was just like when people say no offense before saying something offensive. He was happy to pass the blame to us.

"Thank you for your feedback," Kendra said. "We will think about it. Now, I'll ask you to put aside your belief that everyone in this community is kind and forgiving and think about what you suggested. Who would be so afraid that they'd kill Randi rather than let three protectors do their job."

I looked down to prevent Vijay seeing my smile. Henry was doing the same. Kendra was going to be a wonderful protector.

Vijay, to his credit, closed his eyes and thought. His aura was swirling with irritation and admiration. He liked her confidence and didn't like it pointed at him.

"I suppose if I have to pick names. First Maggie Bell. She's a solitary living near the garden. She's always talking about reinforcing the wards. To hide Raven's Rest from sight. Won't believe us when we tell her it would have the opposite affect. She has the least interaction with the broader community. And, as much as I hate to think it, Alexi. He called you without notifying us. Until you agreed to come that is."

"Thank you," Kendra said.

"Oh, and Felix. He wanted to hack into her cloud account and delete all her video. Said it would solve the problem. Very determined to get his way. But he did back down, so I don't know."

After Vijay left, Kendra took Pickle for a walk to burn off some energy. Henry and I sat in the conference room talking about Vijay's idea of a ritual.

"I think my power will come in handy," Henry said. "When he brought it up, I thought something more. What if there's still a danger and we're not noticing because the murder is taking the attention?"

"The content of her videos is still around," I said. "I don't feel a huge danger to the world, but we don't have the official word that the police are closing the case. And they have her camera which might be just as bad as her publishing. Okay so how do we turn your power to see the consequences into something people can see?"

"Let me try casting projections," he said. "If not, surely someone here has the ability to link with me and make my thoughts visible."

"Are we setting a precedent? Shouldn't people just believe us?" Kendra asked.

Since this was a new concept, I couldn't answer fully. "Wouldn't it be better to have proof? I'll reach out to Mrs. V. Perhaps there's a charm."

It was only mid-morning, and I wanted to keep interviewing people. We would have to find Maggie and if Vijay was right, we needed to reorder our interviews. If the ritual could be done over lunch with the council members in attendance, there wouldn't be much of a delay.

Kendra rejoined us. “I need to go to a pet store because there’s a stupid leash rule and I don’t have one for Pickle. And I totally don’t need one, but a plain human lady gave me a lecture. And I can’t exactly say he’s my familiar and won’t run into traffic or bite someone.”

The thirteen-year-old was back. A relief if I’m honest. We brought her up to date and decided on a break before the next interview.

14

Henry tried to display his predictions, but nothing seemed to work. "I think it is possible, but I have no idea how to trigger it," he said.

"Let's me ask Mrs. V."

I sent a text, and she replied immediately. *Tell your crow to come and get a charm.*

"Am already here," he announced.

Ten minutes later he flew into the lobby and dropped a stone hanging on a leather and string thong into my hand.

"The Henry one just thinks his power and the charm will make it like a movie," he said without any pomp. "I wish to see the new familiar. Tulip has some suggestions for him."

"He is not to be trained as a thug," I said. "Let him be."

"We'll see," Destroyer said. "I have no new information on your killer. I will go myself to ensure my spies are doing a complete survey. The new recruits need some observation and support."

I was going up there myself soon—no not myself, I had a team. "We'll have Randi's belongings soon but there might be other evidence. I don't know what to tell your spies to look for."

"I have charged them to report anything unusual. I will speak to the puppy now."

I shook my head and told Kendra to ignore whatever my crow told her. Thankfully he would have to communicate through Pickle.

Alexi walked into the lobby from the rear entrance. "We are ready for you in the garden. Would you like me to escort you?"

"I need to talk to my colleagues first. We'll be there in five minutes."

I send a text to Kendra and Henry to join me in my room. We needed to decide on the details of the ritual. This was probably going to create a tradition since there was currently nothing about proving a protector's opinion. I hoped the other protectors around the world didn't mind.

Kendra walked in with Pickle close at her heels. He looked up at her as he trotted along and I wondered how he avoided tripping over things in his way. Henry joined us a second behind the two.

"Destroyer," I said pointing to him so the others knew what I was doing. "We need to concentrate. Please keep your conversation with Pickle private for now."

"Why does he want to talk to my familiar?" Kendra asked.

"I don't know. But he can't do anything to him, so it's easier to let them chat."

The puppy turned to face Destroyer and then licked Kendra's hand before trotting off to the window.

I held out the charm by the strap. "This should project your consequence power to visuals, Henry. Can you try before we go into the full ritual?"

He took the charm from me and touched the knot. "Hmm. Similar to a double dragon knot. And I see threads of flax. This is fascinating. Perhaps I will start researching knots when I have some free time. Ask me something that will trigger my power."

"If I let Destroyer talk to Pickle for a long time will it be a good thing," Kendra said. "Sorry, Cossi, I just don't want him to turn into some kind imperial guard."

I laughed at the image that brought to mind. Imperial storm troopers with cute puppy faces.

Henry stared at the knot and three bubbles rose a foot in front of his face.

In the highest one, which I suppose is the most likely, an image of Pickle trotting alongside his witch. The right bubble showed Pickle doing much the same but dressed in a military uniform. The final one, showed Destroyer riding Pickle.

"Those are the images." Henry broke his concentration, and the bubbles disappeared. "How will we interpret the results for the council?"

"Did you choose which ones displayed?" I asked. "Not that I want to manipulate the results but it's important to get context."

"I focused on the three most likely," Henry said. "Would you like to hear my interpretation?"

"In a second," Kendra said. "Here's what I think those predictions mean. In each one Pickle was himself. I didn't feel like Destroyer had any effect. In the one with the clothes, I think Pickle liked the outfit and was wearing it because of that, but also to make the crow happy. In the third one, they seemed to be friends. So not a problem?"

"Well done," Henry said. "Let's hope the ones we're about to do are as clear."

We headed to the back garden of the Gathering House. The council members were sitting on benches around an unlit fire pit. I explained what was going to happen and Marina waved me to start.

"Would Randi's plans have endangered our world if she had continued?" Kendra spoke clearly and then stepped back for Henry to take the stage.

A moment after he muttered the question to the knot, three bubbles appeared.

"Oh no," Alexi gasped the words.

I agreed. All three bubbles showed varying scenes of destruction.

"Well, I suppose that needs no interpretation," Felix said. "None of us doubted that. But is the danger still present? And is there a way to see if Randi was murdered and who did it?"

"It's not usually that specific," Henry said. "Let's start with the first question. Is the danger still there? By that we mean is it still possible that Randi's actions will endanger us?" He waited until the council nodded to make sure the question was acceptable.

This time only two bubbles side by side. One still showed destruction, but on a much smaller scale as if the witches and shifters were able to hide before it got too bad. The other showed what I thought might be a regular day in Raven's Rest.

"So, an equal chance either way," Alexi said. "Perhaps if we solve the case fast it will matter."

"That leads us to the next question," I said. "Was Randi murdered? And if so who did it?"

Henry looked doubtful, but only to me because I could read his emotions. He projected stillness. I wondered if that was because up to now, he'd been overwhelmed with this power.

"One question at a time, I think," he said. "We don't want to confuse the outcome. We know there is still a danger that she has brought a bleak future. Let me ask first if she was killed."

Henry discarded the charm. If I had to guess, Mrs. V had included instructions on using his will instead of a prop.

One bubble rose. Maybe now he had control over the power, he could get it to extrapolate on past events. The bubble showed Randi on the edge of the cliff. Hand out to stop someone out of the scene. Then a branch pushed at her and she was falling.

"I guess that's a yes," Marina said. "Will it tell us who?"

Henry asked the question, but no bubble rose.

"Then I hope you get the killer fast," Alexi said. "I imagine the danger will be gone when your case is solved."

I wasn't sure he was right, but it didn't matter. Even without the power Henry wielded, I could extrapolate that one of our yet to be found clues was going to end the danger.

15

I wanted to talk to Kendra and Henry about the ritual but we had one more scheduled interview with Jorge. He was at the cliffs when the incident happened, and I hoped he'd seen something that would point us to the next clue. This case was the slowest I'd been involved in so far. Maybe it was more like I had the idea that three protector would work faster than one and a cop, but it felt like we'd made no progress at all.

I guess that was true on the murder. The only step forward was we'd found a way to convince people we were right.

We also needed to get out of the Gathering House. I was starting to feel stifled. There was no real need to hold all the interviews here. The community was small and walkable.

Too late to change the one with Jorge. As we waited for him to arrive, I made a mental list—yes another one. We'd confirmed it was real danger for Randi to post her documentary—no brainer. But the case wasn't the only thing we'd accomplished. Henry was more functional thanks to

Kendra. We'd found a way to convince people that the protectors did know what they were doing—something that should never be in question.

Kendra and Pickle had found each other. Perhaps that wouldn't have happened without Randi. And I was starting to suspect Henry needed no training now that he wasn't drowning I possibilities. A good thing in the bigger picture. One more functioning protector was a huge bonus. No matter how quickly Kendra developed her skills, there was only so much a thirteen-year-old could do in the plain world without raising suspicion.

Alexi opened the conference room door and ushered a man inside. "This is Jorge Rodriguez. Let me know if you need me."

The man was short with a strong upper body. His hair was still mostly black even though he looked to be getting closer to sixty than forty. He smiled at us as he took his seat. "I just came from a job," he said. "Sorry I couldn't freshen up. Lela, that's my wife, would be horrified if she knew I came here like this."

He was clean and dressed in work clothes. I didn't see anything wrong with the way he looked.

"You did the right thing," Kendra said. "We need to move this case forward and that's not going to happen if we wait for everyone to dress up."

His smile broadened. I couldn't see anything in his emotions that made me think he could hurt a fly let alone a witch.

"A shield will show you only what he wants," Destroyer announced.

"Thanks for telling me the obvious," I said. "I'll scan him later if I suspect anything."

"The dog will be of help," Destroyer said.

I told him to let me concentrate and his voice receded.

"I was there checking the cliff," Jorge was saying. Kendra must have asked him why he was at the area. "I volunteer, you see. I can see weaknesses in the rock. That's why I'm a stonemason. I build walls and make sure they will last until someone decides to take them down."

"Did you see anyone?" she asked.

"Randi," he said. "I went up to chat with her. She was pointing to something behind her."

There was the first lie. Like every time before, I had no idea what the lie was. But Kendra gave a little nod to let me know she'd noticed.

She didn't let it pass. "Is that really why you went all the way up to where she was killed?" Kendra kept her eyes on Jorge.

"I didn't go all the away up. Not to where she was later. It was just about halfway." The lie was still there.

"What was she pointing at?" Kendra asked.

"Someone had dug into the cliff." He frowned. "No that's not quite right. Not dug exactly. Probably one of the plain humans. They like to try climbing even after reading the warnings. Often they try to put one of those anchor things in. That's what it looked like."

Still not the lie.

"And what did you say?"

"I'd let the council know. That we needed to do the usual repairs. I told her to be careful because there were more places like that, not dug but damaged, then we might see a lot more water coming through. It finds its own way, you know."

"Did you see anyone else?" Kendra asked, digging at the only place the lie could be now.

Jorge closed his eyes and muttered through the morning. Narrating the events to refresh his memory.

"Ah, yes. I met Alexi coming down, or we met him. Randi was there."

So not a lie as much as forgetting. There were spells that could hide a memory. None of them would stand up to a determined attempt to recall like telling yourself what you actually did.

"Did they talk?" Kendra asked. "Like were they nice? or did it sound like they had a fight?"

Jorge startled at the thought. "No. They were friends. Even with the fuss about Randi's plans. They were civil, but not angry."

Kendra's aura spiked a little sky blue disbelief. Jorge must live a very sheltered life, even for a witch, to not understand the level of seething rage that could be hidden behind civility. But I didn't peg Alexi for that kind of passive aggressive behavior, anyway. He was open and welcoming.

"Is there anything else we should know?" Kendra asked. "You left out meeting Alexi before. What else are you hiding?"

Pickle barked but stayed in the corner next to Henry.

"I didn't leave it out," Jorge said affronted. "I forgot. And no. After Alexi passed, I reminded Randi to be careful and headed back to my job."

We weren't going to get anything more from him. I had no worry Kendra's curtness had discouraged him from speaking. He respected the role of protector too much to obstruct us. Or possibly some of that respect was fear. We had other people to interview, and I just hoped that one of them would be different. None of the people we'd met so far had shown they were hiding the fact they were a murderer, or knew who was.

Henry opened the door to let him out and Pickle jumped for the door. Taking off running as fast as his legs would carry him around the entire lobby.

"Someone has the zoomies," Henry said.

"Is he okay?" Kendra asked as she stepped forward to catch him. "Never mind." She started giggling. "He says too much energy. It's itchy and he needs to run away."

We stood and watched as the puppy veered off down the hall toward the back door. Skidding to a halt he flipped and raced back.

"He was right about Jorge," Kendra said.

"He told you something?" I asked. Usually I could hear all the animals, but only because they didn't think to block me. This puppy was smart. I was more than grateful he didn't share his excess energy with me.

"I listened to him the whole time," she said. "Jorge lied, right? Shouldn't we arrest him?"

"He said he couldn't remember," Henry said. "I believe him, but you have the truth power. What did that tell you?"

He was turning out to be a great co-mentor. His question reinforced my idea he'd be independent when this case was done—probably was now.

"Okay, yes, he thought he was telling the truth," she said after a pause. "My power picked up the forgetting thing, but nothing else. Do you think the killer spelled him to forgetting?"

"It's possible," I said. "But even if that's right, we can't force him to fight it. I suspect he'll do some thinking and let us know. He wants this solved and life back to normal."

"Yeah, but remember the ritual said there's still danger," Kendra said.

"We have no clues on that either," Henry said. "We still

have Maggie to interview, but then I think a visit to the site of the murder would be in order. Yes?"

His words made me wonder why we hadn't already gone there. I dismissed the thought, the case was all over the place. Destroyer's spies were looking. It's not like we were ignoring it.

16

The problem with arranging interviews ahead of time was you were stuck on that schedule. Nothing we learned could distract us. What I wanted to do was get to the cliffs and do my own search. Destroyer's army could easily miss something because they didn't know what to look for.

"This Maggie person,"Kendra said. "Am I interviewing? Or do you want someone else to have a go?"

"Are you tired?" Henry asked. "That last one was difficult."

"Not tired," she said. "Maybe bored. Mostly I feel like I need to pay more attention to Pickle."

The puppy barked and said, "yes. I must be with my witch, and I need a walk, and I will need to mark my territory."

"This isn't where you'll be living," I said.

He sat and looked at me. "It is my territory for now."

"Okay, this is the last one for today," I said. "I hope it will be early enough to go to the site before dark."

"I'll take the interview," Henry said. "I'll rely on both of you to advise me if she lies."

Alexi joined us giving Pickle a few scritches behind his ears. "I received a call from Maggie," he said. "She asked that you come to her if possible."

There was a lie somewhere. Kendra looked up from Pickle and gave him one of those teenage stares that seemed to come from deep in their bodies, part 'I don't care' and part accusation.

"Why did you lie?" she asked.

Alexi gave a polite cough. "I paraphrased. Maggie tends to be, I suppose blunt is the nice way of saying it. I can demand she come here, if you prefer."

"Where does she live?" Henry asked.

"Just a little way from the Impossible Garden. I can drive you."

"And is there a path from the garden to the cliff path?" I asked. We might be able to accomplish three things at once.

"It's a good walk, but the path is clear," he said. "I can stay and guide you."

"I think we'll manage," I said. Having Alexi escort us around was starting to feel a bit claustrophobic. "Kendra can give Pickle some exercise while we talk to Maggie."

ALEXI STOPPED the car at the end of a driveway. "If you follow that, Maggie's place is at the end. Only a few minutes, don't worry. I can drop Kendra closer to the garden. A better place for Pickle to run."

"I'm going with them, thanks anyway," Kendre slid out of the back seat Pickle under her arm.

Henry led the way up the drive. It took a left turn after a couple of minutes, and then Maggie's house came into view.

A rustic cabin, all wood, with a shingle roof almost completely covered in moss.

The door opened and witch stepped out. Maggie looked as old as Mrs. V. Her hair was loose and floated like a white puffball. There was nothing aged about her posture, or her face. Without my powers, I might have thought she was furious at us for interrupting. The splash of nosiness, and excitement in her aura told me she was more interested than annoyed.

She invited us into her kitchen for the usual tea and cookies. When we were seated, she turned from the kettle to say, "I didn't do it. I don't know anything. Why are you interrupting my day?"

Henry waved her to the chair. "We will make this quick. You might have some detail that leads us to another clue. We are talking to a lot of people."

She wasn't appeased, and I hoped she wouldn't draw the interview out with obstructions.

Pickle barked once and settled under the table on Kendra's feet.

"What could I know,' Maggie said picking a carrot out of a basket of produce and putting it down for Pickle. ""I sit in my cabin researching or developing my stories."

No lie or delay so far.

"What stories?" Henry asked. I guess he was trying to break her defense.

"I make up stories and my magic brings them to life. I perform here. People love them. I watched some of those Telenovelas and found the trick to keep the audience hooked. You should follow my witchtube channel."

Well that sparked her to life. And she was smarter than Randi. Keeping the videos away from the plain humans even though she could make a ton of money from ads. And was in no danger of exposing us.

"You never thought to put them on a plain human platform?" Henry asked as if he'd read my thoughts.

"Randi said I should. But it's not like selling our jewelry or wine on line," Maggie said. "Get some success in entertaining and some big company wants to buy you out. Too risky."

Pickle hopped onto Kendra's lap still crunching the carrot. I heard him say he wanted a walk. Kendra promised him soon and held him there.

"She said I was being selfish," Maggie continued unprompted. "Our last conversation was a fight. Well, you can't fix the past. Still think I'm right."

No lies in her answers. I started to tell her we had enough when Henry asked his next question.

"Is the community in need of cash?"

"You'll have to ask the council," Maggie said. "No signs of it but like I said, I stay in my cabin."

"Who do you think might have killed her?"

Kendra stood. "I have to take Pickle out."

When she was gone, Henry repeated his question.

"I know you've talked to people who think she was a problem all her life. But she was just passionate about knowledge and misguided about risk. I can't believe anyone in Raven's Rest would kill, but apparently someone has. My thought is someone on council."

"Why?" Henry asked.

"Most to lose," Maggie said. "Their job to protect us. If she exposed the community, their reputations are gone. We'd do our best to make the plains believe we were the only witches around, but it would be their job. The council, I mean."

It didn't seem like a motive to me. Of course, as I thought back on the Vancouver council and the one in Germany, maybe being in the middle of the plain humans meant you needed to be harsh.

"If you'll give us a moment," Henry said. "I need to confer with my colleague."

He led me outside the cottage door.. "Did I miss a signal she was lying?"

"No. She told the truth."

"Her comment about the council was interesting. Do you want me to pursue it?"

"It certainly gives us something to follow up later, but I think we can let her go. There's time to look at the crime scene before it gets too late."

"We will wait for Kendra?"

I thought about his insistence on his territory marking, and the fact he was a puppy. And that we'd be on a path half way up the cliff. "I'll text her to say we'll go to the cliffs. She can spend the afternoon bonding. A long walk back to the Gathering House might be the best thing for Pickle."

Maggie thanked us for not wasting her time. "I can call someone to pick you up," she said. "The road isn't safe to just walk, and the paths through the forest can be confusing."

I thought at Destroyer to make sure Kendra and Pickle didn't get lost.

"We are planning to visit the path Randi fell from. How will we get there," Henry asked. "Cossi isn't dressed for a hike."

I should have let our ride wait, we'd only been with Maggie for fifteen minutes. "I can call Alexi," I said.

"I am tied up right now," Alexi said. "Perhaps tomorrow morning?"

So we didn't even have a ride back. "I'll find someone else. Thanks."

Maggie suggested Vijay. "He's the one who knows the cliffs best."

In the end Vijay agreed to meet us in thirty minutes out front of Maggie's.

Time for me to get ready, although I didn't bring anything suitable.

"I can arrange a delivery," Destroyer said. No imperial tone evident. "Communicate to your friend to leave a bundle of clothing and an eagle will bring it."

I thanked him and texted Lilibeth to leave my hiking boots and a long-sleeved tee shirt where Destroyer instructed then drop them in Maggie's front yard.

"Have your army found anything?" I asked.

"I am informed that there is a new path down that was created when she fell," he said. "I am bringing the local beasts into the empire, so I have not monitored closely."

That explained his distraction. If he was successful, maybe we should be talking about his network of spies keeping an eye on the area.

My clothes arrived faster than I expected. The eagle, like they all do, said he was not a taxi service and flew away.

I took the bundle inside and opened it in Maggie's bathroom. Lilibeth had tied everything together with one of the throws I kept in my bedroom. A note said, *a little something to remind you of home.*

17

Vijay looked up the path and took a deep breath. "I've been up there so many times before, but now, it feels very different."

"Would you like to stay here?" Henry asked. "We can go ourselves."

Vijay looked around at the trees surrounding the trailhead and then back up the path. "No. It will give me an opportunity to pay respects. We should be there in fifteen minutes or so."

Ten minutes later I was applauding myself for leaving Kendra and Pickle behind. The path was just wide enough for two people to pass. If someone was on their way down, we'd all have to press into the cliff face to allow them past. A rambunctious puppy would be a danger.

"Do you know where the hole is that Jorge found?" I asked. "He said it looked like someone was attempting to place a climbing anchor."

"I didn't realize," Vijay said. "I know what they look like, so I'll point it out when we pass."

It didn't take long. The hole was really subtle. I wouldn't

have noticed it, but I wasn't local. A witch from Raven's Rest would likely notice a new leaf on a weed. It wasn't really a hole, anyway. Two large sections of the cliff met, leaving a triangular space—small enough that I was only able to put two fingers inside. The edges were smoothed as though something had been hammered in and then removed.

"No water," Henry said. "Jorge told us the little streams inside the rock would find the outlet."

Vijay leaned in to check for himself. "Not here. The streams are farther up. I'll make a note to have the signs updated at the entrance. No climbing. Although the plain humans seem to take it as a challenge rather than a warning."

"Perhaps a ward?" I said. "To turn away someone intent on ignoring the sign?"

"Yes," Vijay said. "We try to keep the wards to a minimum. Don't want to raise anyone's curiosity. I suppose we might have erred too much on the side of caution."

We continued up. Destroyer reported that his spies were flying around the area. I could direct them if I needed. He also told me Kendra was on her way back to the Gathering House, led by a deer.

We finally stopped at a slight widening of the path here a few rocks jutted over the edge almost like a barrier. Turning to the rock face, I saw the weeping holes, and wet patches. Right now, they were only on the vertical surface, but it was easy to imagine morning dew and run off making a dangerous mix.

The image of someone using a branch to push Randi over ran in my mind. What if her camera caught that? "Did the police return her equipment?"

"Yes, the SD card was missing," Vijay said. "The police

think it was knocked out as she... bounced." He blinked away moisture in his eyes.

"I need to look down," I said. "Can you anchor me?" I figured Destroyer would send an eagle to catch me if the worst happened, but it wasn't worth the risk.

"I'll do it," Henry said. "Just hang onto my belt. What are you hoping to see?"

"No. I am the lightest. If we don't have a rope, I can wear your belt."

"I can go and get ropes," Vijay said.

"You will not endanger yourself!" Destroyer screamed in my head.

I forgot the effect my death would have on him. Not that I was willing to die. "Okay. Everyone stop. My familiar doesn't want this either. But I have a better idea."

I sent out a call to any animals or birds in the area. Within minutes two starlings and a family of mice arrived.

"I need to find something that might have dropped while the witch fell," I said in my mind.

"We can climb down," the largest mouse said. "How big is the thing?"

"We can survey and guide," one of the starlings said.

I formed my fingers in to a square about the size of an SD card then realized it might be smaller. "Can you tell the color of something?"

"Some," the starling said.

"Yes," the mouse said.

I described an SD card. The color, the row of metal pieces, and a few more possible sizes. The birds swooped away from us and then down. The mice simply scampered between the rocks and disappeared.

"Will they be of any use?" Vijay asked. "They are wild

and... well. I suppose they are so small I'm not sure I understand how they can compete a complex assignment."

I remembered how I'd felt the first time I spoke to an animal. Surprised I could make sense of it even knowing I had the power. "You'll see," I said. "Animals have helped me a lot since I learned I was a witch. Small and wild doesn't mean stupid."

"I can't see the mice," Henry said. He was looking over the edge. Standing far enough away that he wasn't in danger. "The birds are doing vertical loops. It's fascinating."

I told myself he was safe, but I had to look away. "Why would Randi have come up here?" I asked more to myself than either of the others.

"The view is quite something," Henry said. "You can see past where Henbane would be if it was visible."

"Oh, yeah, she was taking some establishing shots," I said. "It's certainly beautiful. I'm surprised the tourist board doesn't show the area from here."

I turned away from the view and started looking for damage to the cliff face. Nothing like what we'd seen coming up, but there were several wet lines, like the stone was weeping. "Is it like this all year round?"

"Yes." Vijay pointed upward. "Higher, the water is less apparent, and in winter, the leaking is held back by ice. Randi would have been very careful."

"I'm sure she was, but you saw the image," Henry said. "She was pushed."

Vijay nodded. "That is true. Let's hope your animals find the recording and it shows more than the branch."

"Wait," I said taking a careful step back so I could get a better look around me. "Where did the branch come from?"

There were no roots, or crooked trees in reach.

"It wasn't done in the passion of the moment," Vijay said, his voice hushed.

"I don't remember seeing any place near this spot to break off a branch," I said. "Whoever did this brought the weapon with them."

Vijay looked at me, his face and aura filled with horror. "Someone came here to kill Randi? No. It's not possible that anyone in Raven's Rest would do such and evil thing."

He must be innocent, or a very good actor with a strong shield.

"It is possible that was not the original plan," Henry said. "I can easily see other options even without my power. What we saw as a branch, could be a rustic walking stick. Or it came from higher up. Our killer was carrying it down the path so it wouldn't fall and injure someone. It had washed down to this point and now it's down the side of the cliff."

"Right," I said. "Thank you for bringing us back to reality. We can't just jump on a clue and run with it."

The starlings flashed by. "The mice are coming. We must go to the dusk rising."

I wished them luck.

The largest mouse was the first over the ledge. He spat an SD card at my feet.

"Thank you," I said, reaching into my pocket for the usual payment I kept there.

"Tell the crow we helped," he said jumping on the seeds. "Or he said we would be banished."

"No banishing," I said aloud and to Destroyer in my mind.

18

"Felix will be able to help," Vijay said. "I'll call when we get to the bottom. I want my attention on the path, not the phone."

It was starting to get dark as we made our way down, how had the day slipped away? The sun still lighting the upper trail was blocked by the cliff and the trees. I was behind Vijay and Henry brought up the rear. I could hear the rustling of small animals in the undergrowth as we stepped into the clearing. The dusk animals were about their business.

Vijay stood a short distance away making his call.

"We can interview Felix while he looks at the card," Henry said. "Kendra will miss out, but that can't be helped."

"The interviews haven't really helped," I said. "But we might be doing them again when we see what she was filming."

Vijay returned before Henry could respond.

"Now is a good time," he said. "I'll drop you off at his house. It's only a short walk from there to the Gathering House."

"What did you tell him?" I realized too late that we couldn't afford rumors about what we'd found.

"Only that we found the card and it's damaged."

That could be bad enough. "You can't tell anyone else. We don't want the murderer hearing we might have proof."

He looked insulted. "I mentioned that to Felix, Protector."

We piled into the car. Vijay drove in silence to a small house a few blocks from the Gathering House. It was an alpine style with a big A frame around the door. The beam was black and the rest of the house was a very light cream. Dramatic and still inviting. The front door opened and Felix stepped out.

"Come along. We'll go to my work room. I have tea and snacks. Is the youngest not with you?"

"She's getting to know her new familiar," Henry said. "Tea would be lovely."

Vijay waved goodbye from the car and drove off. I tried not to fret about him spreading rumors. He'd seen the danger without my asking that he keep quiet. He wasn't crossed off my list, but I didn't really think he was our killer.

I made a quick check-in on Kendra. "They are almost home," Destroyer said. "I applaud my imperial guides."

Felix ushered us through the house into a back bedroom. Well at one time it was a bedroom, but now it was filled with monitors and laptops. The closet held shelves of random equipment. The blinds on the windows were blocking out any ambient light.

"I have a little power that might help us right away," Felix said. "Put the card on the desk please."

I handed it to Henry who placed it between two keyboards.

Felix stroked his chin and stared at it.

"What will your power tell you?" Henry asked. "Can you read the files?"

"No." Felix was deep in thought and the word seemed to come from a different place. "I can tell if the effort to clean it will result in information. Randi backed up to the cloud, but manually. Her camera wasn't internet enabled."

I wanted to ask a long list of questions about the card, about Randi, about whether he'd killed her. If he was the killer we wouldn't find any evidence.

"I think it is worth it," he said finally. "We will clean the outside so it will go into the drive and see what we see."

Instead of using a cloth to remove the debris, Felix placed a sheet of paper beside the card and drew a line with violet powder from the one object to the other.

"Please don't speak when I trigger the spell. Don't want to distract the magic."

I held my breath. He muttered some words in fake Latin, nonsense words. And then the power moved. It was creepy. Like a snake appeared beneath the powder and was slithering its way out. Then the spell touched the first crusted mud. The dirt broke up and made its way along the powder to the paper. No longer like a snake, more like ants carrying home a treasure.

In a few minutes, the SD card looked almost new. The paper was covered in fragments of mud, seeds, and a few tiny pebbles.

"I will try it now," Felix said reaching for the card. "The inside may not have suffered much damage. Fingers crossed."

He touched a key on the closest laptop bringing it to life. He inserted the card gently and sat. "So far so good."

The video app he pulled up started with a grainy view over the ocean. Then Randi's voice came through.

"Absolutely not."

A second voice came in. This one not clear, crying and affected by the damage. "Randi… you must see…"

"Who is that?" Henry asked.

"I can't tell anymore than you can," Felix said. "It is familiar, but I think Randi pointed the mic toward herself. She would have been narrating the images."

"Male," I said. "That helps. Any indication of the time?" Felix might see something we wouldn't notice as strangers.

"I agree it's male, and I can't tell you who, but as I said, it feels familiar. I'll have to do more work to clear the debris, but the metadata will tell us when the recording happened."

"How long will that take?" I asked. To be honest, I was hungry, and we still had to ask him the interview questions. My phone vibrated, and I looked down to see Kendra's had been sending texts for the last five minutes.

"Several hours, I think," Felix said. "I will start the process now, but when it is clean, I will use technology because it is much more effective than magic for this kind of thing. When it is set up, we should have tea, yes?"

He took a tray from the closet of odd devices and sat it on a stool Then he placed the SD card inside. Finally adding a liberal coat of the powder with a tail leading to the far side of the tray, he said the words again.

"I will not sleep until we have a result." He ushered us to the kitchen. The sun was almost set, but the sky was painted in shades of orange and pink like a celebration of a well lived day.

"You must call whenever that happens. Do not worry about the hour," Henry said. "But now I think is a good time to ask our questions."

"An interview? Yes. Of course without all the details how will you find justice. Settle down and we can talk over refreshments."

The tea was ginger lemon, the cookies dark chocolate with bits of dried cherry. My stomach stopped complaining.

"I'll just set the recorder and we can get started," Henry said.

I settled in a chair to the side so Felix wouldn't be distracted by my presence. And I could munch on the treats.

He happily answered the questions about where he was, providing Henry with the names of two people who could confirm his alibi. "Of course, that confirms theirs as well. That is efficient."

"What did you think of Randi's plans?" Henry asked.

"Well, since I saw your excellent imagery, I have changed my mind," Felix said. "Before, I though she was a little rash, but isn't it inevitable? That something will fail in our wards. Henbane only recently sent out the spell to mitigate the selfies and other irritating plain human behavior."

"An interesting question. Did you think we could live in harmony with the plain humans?"

Henry's voice was calm which I had to admire. He was boiling with fear and his control of the power was slipping. What the heck was Felix thinking?

"If properly managed," Felix said. "Not the way Randi was going about it. With preparation and a clear communication strategy."

Henry tipped his head as if he was interested. "And now?"

"Your prediction was clear, but it was based on Randi's action. Perhaps there is still hope."

"You say the walls are eroding," Henry said. "Perhaps that is why more protectors are coming into their power?"

Felix's eyes widened in surprise. I sipped my tea trying not to call him an idiot even in my mind.

"You bring up a good point," Felix said. "I have much to think on."

We left him with a reminder to keep this quiet and call us when he had news.

19

The next morning I tried to put aside my frustration at still not catching the killer. I reminded myself of what we'd accomplished. We'd done a lot to convince the community that Randi's plans were dangerous. We'd found a clue that didn't tell us much—yet. Part of me said that I should stop worrying and just keep plugging at the investigation. That I had two people to help me. That the danger was minimal now. Another part of me was scared that somehow Randi had set up her documentary to publish without her interaction.

On top of all that, Kendra was due back at school in a couple of days and I felt like I was shortchanging her protector training.

Kendra knocked on my door and stuck her head in. "I've walked Pickle and he's agreed to behave today. Come for breakfast."

Having her familiar hadn't helped our investigation yesterday. I expected him to jump and growl at the killer. He hadn't but was it because the killer hadn't been near us? Or was I asking too much of a puppy?

"The Pickle dog is capable," Destroyer said. "He has already agreed to become my ambassador to the pet universe when the valiant warrior Kendra is fully trained."

"That will be a while," I said. "Not that she won't learn fast, but teenagers are not expected to travel alone. To be a protector, she'll need to fly places, and get her driver's license, and meet a whole lot of plain human requirements."

"Assign her an adult." The words were definitely an order. "Should she need an escort, any witch will do."

I hadn't thought about that option. Kendra still had some maturing to do, but maybe only a couple of years if we worked during her school breaks. If she move to Henbane, maybe not even a year. "Good idea, emperor."

Henry and Kendra were talking over toast and fruit at the small table for guests. I picked out a muffin and poured from a carafe labeled 'brightness tea'. Anything that gave me an edge was welcome.

"Good morning," Henry said. "No news from Felix?"

I hadn't checked my phone yet. I'd missed two texts. One from Mark asking if we needed him and one from Felix. *Progress made. Not clear enough yet. Possibly by dinner time.*

I responded to Mark with *no, thanks for asking*, and Felix with *let us know as soon as it's ready.*

"Then we have two interviews before we run out of suspects," Henry said.

Kendra checked her list. "No. We have three, Carmen, Marina, and Alexi. We should have done him earlier like we planned, but you went to the cliff."

"I guess it feels like we've already interviewed him," I said. "He's been so helpful. I think we need to get out of here and meet more of our suspects in their homes."

"It will give us a chance to see the neighborhood," Henry

said. "I've picked out a map of where everyone and everything is around here. We can walk to Carmen's house. Then it's a bit longer to Marina's."

"Pickle will need a walk by then, so that's great." Kendra patted his head and called him a good boy.

Perhaps it was much better that Destroyer chose me. I wasn't much of a dog person, although crows could be cuddlier.

"Then Alexi," Henry said. "I suggest we give some thought to our next steps as we travel between our suspects."

"I'll text everyone and line them up," I said.

"No need," Henry said holding up his phone. "Carmen is expecting us within the hour. Marina will wait to hear before we leave. I scheduled Alexi for after lunch. There's a nice pub between Marina's and Alexi's where we can chat."

I really needed to work on my expectations of this team. Henry was doing a great job of being a protector without any pointers. "Thanks, that's perfect. I think we have time to talk a little about mentoring."

"You are doing a great job," Kendra said. "We don't have time for testing, right? Maybe when we get back to Henbane?"

Anxiety flooded her usual brightly eager emotions. Pickle gave me a cute puppy growl for upsetting his witch.

"No tests," I said. "A check-in. This case has given us each the chance to show what we know. I don't want to waste your time with made up scenarios if we can just take advantage of the opportunity."

"Thank you, Cossi," Henry said. "Is there a gap you see? Something I need to learn in particular?"

This was tricky because I didn't want Kendra to feel left out and hurt. But better to be clear than try to protect her feelings. "Henry, I think you are pretty much ready. I'd like to know if you have something you want to focus on?"

"When I first realized I had these powers, I was afraid. You saw how overwhelmed I was at the start. Kendra's skill at providing me a control switch has freed me."

"When we're done here, we can talk about how you step into a working protector role. Kendra, what do you think you need?"

"I wish I could say nothing," she said. "Look, I'm thirteen, it would be crazy to think I can handle the job on my own. My familiar is a baby. I think I need everything. I want to interview people so I get better at reading them."

"Then we'll let you do that," I said. "Don't worry about asking us for help, like you said, you're young. When we're back on Henbane, we'll make a plan."

That settled, we headed out to Carmen and, with luck, a clue that will close the case.

THE HOUSE COULD HAVE BEEN in any development from thirty years ago. Houses that would have been cookie cutter at the beginning. But being owner witches meant the subsequent years had brought changes. Carmen's house was a bright yellow with white trim, and flowering plants leading to the front door.

She opened the door as Kendra reached up to knock.

"Come on in," she said. "We'll sit on the patio. It's still warm enough during the day. I love the sound of the birds, don't you?"

The patio was a wide paved section outside the kitchen door. The pavers were arranged in a spread of a peacock's tail. A wrought iron patio set stood near a bird bath and three feeders. A pair of humming birds were fighting over the best place to sip nectar. Their voices were high, as you would expect, and fast. I could only catch a word or two and it was all about who got to sip first.

"Ask whatever you need to," Carmen said when we were seated. "I did not kill Randi. I often thought of it, but I would never actually do it."

Kendra put a notebook on the table along with her phone. She said she'd be recording. Carmen waved a hand as if dismissing all concerns.

"Why did you think of killing Randi?"

"Oh to the point. I like that. Have you ever encountered someone who was determined to start a fight over trivial things? How annoying it can be?" She didn't wait for an answer. "That was Randi. I'm sure others have said the same. Don't get me wrong, she had some great ideas. That impossible garden? I thank her for every fresh avocado. But then she applies that same attitude to something so dangerous."

"Did you tell her what you thought?"

"Of course, dear. We all did. She wouldn't hear it. I suppose we hoped that she would never complete the videos. When I tell you she couldn't let anything go, it applied to herself too. She took up painting. Lot's of talent and no sense of when to call a picture finished."

"But it got to the point that Alexi called a protector," Kendra said.

"Yes. Because we learned she was almost finished," Carmen said. "We discussed using spells to prevent her from going near the plain human platforms, but Felix said nothing would work."

That was new information. If they'd tried at the beginning of the project, Randi might have been distracted. She was too invested by the time the council decided to act.

I kept my attention split between listening the answers, and assessing Kendra's performance. We both knew that Carmen didn't lie about killing Randi, so the questions were headed in a different direction.

"Who do you think might have been so scared that they killed her?"

"Now that's a good question. I've been thinking about it since we saw the images. Where it looked like someone pushed Randi."

Kendra made a note and nodded for Carmen to continue.

"Perhaps it was an accident," Carmen said. "Now I know we all saw the same thing, but we don't know if Randi was already falling and the branch was being offered to pull her back."

"Interesting. I remember it looked very much like a push," Kendra said. "If it was an accident, who do you think was there with her?"

"It could be anyone," Carmen said. "I know you want me to tell you a name, but I can't be sure. I think it is more likely to be someone close to her. They went up there when she was alone. A friend might do that to try one more appeal. A place where she wouldn't feel humiliated if she decided to stop."

Kendra closed her notebook and thanked Carmen. "We might have more questions, but you've been helpful."

Henry sent a text to Marina who was our next subject. She suggested a walk on the beach rather than coming to her home.

20

The beach was the typical gray sand with rocks and logs strewn about. Kendra unclipped Pickle's leash and let him run. Watching the puppy race along the stretch, jumping over the logs and sniffing in tide pools made me smile. And also feel really old. When did I lose that capacity for joy?

"He will not remain a puppy," Destroyer reminded me. "Being my witch puts the resources of the entire empire at your disposal."

In the long term that was true, but right now, I was happy to be entertained by his antics, and happy I didn't have to clean him up.

Marina joined us a few minutes after we arrived. She brought dog treats and human cookies. "It always invigorates me to be here," she said. "Like all the distractions and worries get blown out to the ocean. Of course, it ruins my hair but I don't care."

My own head of curls was streaming out behind me. I'd have to wash it to get out the snarls, but I felt the calming effect too.

"Let's sit," Kendra said pointing to a log. "I can keep an eye on Pickle, but he needs a good run. Yesterday was great, but I don't know how many hour long hikes I have in me."

Marina pulled a blanket out of her huge tote bag and we sat in a row. Kendra next to Marina, me on one side Henry on the other.

"Hang on," Kendra said. "The wind is nice and all, but we won't be able to talk."

She looked behind me and frowned. Then she waved her hand and suddenly the air was calm. "The barrier will go when we leave, but that's nicer, right?"

Marina shook out her hair. It didn't do much good. She had the same kind of curls as me, tight and easily tangled.

"So you want to know if I killed Randi? Or if I know who did?"

"Yes, and maybe some more," Kendra said. "So did you kill her?"

Marina laughed. "Has anyone tried to lie to you about that?"

"Not successfully," Kendra said. "We have lie detecting power, and I guess people know that."

"The witches with that power usually end up as the community police," Marina said. "But you are protectors. Is it different? Others just know a lie, but not what."

Well, Kendra needed to be tested, and she knew it. I couldn't put aside the suspicion that Marina was trying to find out how to avoid telling us. Well, not looking for a way, she already knew skirting the question worked. I pressed my lips together to stop from taking over.

Kendra leaned in a little closer to Marina as if they were friends sharing secrets. "It doesn't matter, really. Did you kill her?"

"No. And I don't know who did."

Truth. Were we going to have to line up every resident and ask that question until we found the liars?

Kendra didn't react to what I knew she was feeling, disappointment. Not that she thought Marina was our killer, just the fact another interview didn't help. "Thank you. Look, you saw the images. There's no doubt someone pushed her over the edge. You must have a guess."

Marina looked out over the water. She wouldn't see Henbane because of the wards. But maybe the sight of the waves and sky would help her think.

Pickle ran up to Kendra and put his paws on her knee. She took out a to-go container and poured some water into the attached bowl. He slurped away at it then moved to Marina.

"Oh you are a pretty boy," Marina said. She held out two treats for him to take, making him sit and beg.

Pickle sat on Kendra's shoes to crunch the treats.

"Would you like something sweet, too," Marina asked holding out cookies filled with seeds and dried fruit. "I promise I won't make you do a trick."

We all laughed. She was a master of diverting attention. I couldn't tell if it was her personality, or some tactic to avoid Kendra's questions.

"Thanks, but maybe after we've finished," Kendra said. "Have you thought of someone?"

"What have others said? I'm not really comfortable pointing the finger. I'm the newest resident. I came here from the east coast ten years ago. Not that I agreed with Randi, of course not. But I'm not sure I'm the right person to give you good information."

"Don't worry about it," Kendra said. "Look I'm a teenager, you can see that. I'm pretty experienced with people gossiping and making up facts. I know how to keep a secret. Just tell us who and why you think they are guilty."

I saw her push a little persuasion power along with her words. The protector power was working. This was important.

Marina sighed. "Fine, you're right. This is important. I did see the vision you created, Henry. Someone definitely pushed Randi. And they were arguing. Too bad the vision wasn't from Randi's perspective. This would all be settled right now."

We all waited. I had no intention of letting her know about the SD card.

"Yes. So two people argued the most with Randi. Quinn and Alexi. I don't think either of them are killers, but obviously that's a false assumption because someone here is. I think it must be someone who was willing to fight with her in public. Most of us tried to talk her out of her plans in private. I mean, embarrassing her was more likely to make Randi hold her ground."

"We heard Randi caused problems all the time," Kendra said. "Why do you think this is different?"

"The danger. The fact she didn't see the problem with exposing us was baffling. I considered moving on, but the repercussions wouldn't just be to Raven's Rest. And how do we know the wards on Henbane would hold if plain humans learned the truth? And not just Henbane. The world."

"I guess that explains it," Kendra said. "I hadn't thought that magic itself would start to fail."

"And there's still a danger, right?" Marina said. "Will that go away when you catch the killer?"

Marina was very good at asking questions. With the pressure of the murder, I hadn't thought through the continuing danger enough. And there would be no answers to Marina's most important point, would magic fail.

Pickle raced off for one more sweep of the beach and pools as soon as Kendra thanked Marina.

"He's going to be very dirty," Henry said. "Does anyone have a spell or charm to clean him up?"

Kendra shook her head. "I can wash him, but that's a really good idea, Henry."

She called Pickle to our side. He was in need of a bath, sand was packed into his double coat. The worst part was he'd found something dead to roll in.

"Maybe we should have Alexi meet us at the Gathering House," Henry said. "Having a rancid dog at an interview might not be ideal."

Kendra laughed and looked at Pickle who was delighted with himself. "That cleaning spell is going on the top of my list."

21

Alexi agreed to meet us after lunch at the Gathering House. We decided a lunch at the pub would be best with a stinky dog. One who was enthusiastically trotting along, proud of his state, and marking territory.

Kendra look at her familiar with a mix of fondness and exasperation. "If we can't sit on the patio, we won't stick around. Pickle needs to be cleaned and he's more important."

The alternative of leaving him tied up outside was not okay. Partly because he'd find a way to escape and come inside.

The pub was only a five-minute walk and they must have some experience with dogs and beaches because to the right of the front door was a tub, a tap, and soap. A sign read, let them shake dry, or come in and get a towel.

Kendra dumped Pickle in the tub and turned on the tap. "Hey this is warm. These people are so cool. I'll clean him up and join you. Can you order me a burger?"

"Yes, no problem. It's warm enough so we'll sit on the

patio," I said. "We'll have privacy to talk, and no one needs to inhale wet dog."

I ordered a burger too, Henry went for fish and chips. I added a soda for Kendra, beer for me and Henry.

"We'll bring it out," the waiter said. "And a few scraps for the puppy."

This was the kind of thing I'd learned to expect from a witch community. Friendly, caring, and inclusive. Randi had done more than endanger the world—okay that was a lot—she'd potentially tainted Raven's Rest with suspicion and fear. That would be gone when the case was solved. I hoped.

We settled at the table, the sun just warm enough that we didn't need the heaters turned on, and waited for our lunch.

"Let's think about this," I said. "So many people have put Alexi on the list of possibles, we have to be careful."

"Because he might not be the killer," Kendra said. "Because he's been so helpful to us, we might not think clearly about him. And he called in the protectors, so people here might be mad at him for doing it."

"It's never that easy," Henry said. "I know I've lived among plain humans for a long time so I might be out of touch. Do most witches still think the plains are bad, simply because they don't have magic. Or are we more open minded?"

"So? What if we are still judgmental? A plain human didn't kill Randi," Kendra said. She bit into her burger and chewed while she waited for his answer.

I decided to let them work it out. My burger was juicy and full of flavor. The fries were crispy and sprinkled with Parmesan cheese. Yes, I wanted the opportunity to observe my protectors, but I couldn't deny I wanted to enjoy my food.

"So, we don't see ourselves as flawed like they are," Henry said. "Despite the fact that someone here is a murderer, no one really has an idea who might have done it. Witches don't kill. Even when someone admits the image showed it is possible, they can't let go."

I had a lot of experience that told me how untrue that statement was. But maybe here, in this community it was the case.

"But we are better," Kendra said handing Pickle a bite of her meat. "Plain humans mostly act like they have to win at everything and they don't seem to mind killing people, or even really hurting them."

"In school, do you mix with the plain human students?" Henry asked. I liked his approach. He could have said, you'll understand when you get older. I imagine Kendra would have reacted like any thirteen-year-old. But he was leading her to the understanding and figuring it out would make her remember the lesson.

"Not really. It's kind of hard when you can't invite plain friends over without a lot of notice."

"What do you think they are like?"

"They gossip and bully and lie, and..." Kendra stopped. "You know like they are all broken into different groups. Mean girls, jocks, nerds."

Henry nodded and took a bite of his fish. The pause let Kendra finish her meal and I could tell she was trying to figure out what point he was making.

Henry decided she needed a nudge. "Okay. Do your friends gossip?"

"Not meanly," Kendra said. "And we're all kinds of kids. I guess witches are better at accepting differences because we don't all get the same powers."

"How did your friends react when you told them you were a protector?"

Kendra's emotions darkened. "First they didn't believe me. Then they teased me. Then I left so I don't know. But we still text. I hope they got over it." Her emotions told me she understood the point but resisted accepting it.

"Just like plain humans," Henry said. "If you think we are better, or not just witches, shifters too. Then you will miss something one day. As a protector."

She sat back with her soda and thought while we finished our lunches. It was a hard lesson to learn for anyone, but thirteen was pretty young to start seeing the world in shades rather than absolutes.

"Let's talk about how we'll interview Alexi," I said to change the subject.

"Just ask him if he killed her," Kendra said. "Then we know what to do."

"But won't you only know if he lies," Henry said. "Assuming he doesn't confess. What if he says no, but because he's convinced himself it was an accident. Will you power see that as a lie?"

"Mine might not," I said.

"I don't know," Kendra said.

"What if he says yes, because he knows the real killer and wants to protect them?"

Kendra rolled her eyes. "Jeez, I thought it would be easier having lie detector power. So I guess the answer is no."

Henry chuckled. "No power is ever easy. When the plain humans use a lie detecting machine, what do they do? Do they ask first if the person is guilty? I only know from books or television."

"Oh, no. They need to get, what's it called? Like they

need to be sure when they are telling the truth before they can recognize the lie?"

"Exactly," Henry sounded proud of her.

"So can I question him?" Kendra stacked our plates. "Or should I watch and learn?"

I looked at Henry hoping he'd give me a hint based on his consequence power, but he simply shrugged.

"Do you think you can do it?" I asked.

"Yes, but I don't know if I'm right. Like, the others were not so important. I figured we were just asking questions. But Alexi is the last one. If I make a mistake, we have to start all over again."

"You can do this," I said. "Alexi is probably not our killer. But he will know more about who might be. And he called us in, so you're dealing with someone who recognized the danger early on. Think about how you've conducted the other interviews. You've pulled out information. You don't always ask right away if they are guilty. Keep in mind what Henry said and I think you'll be fine."

She patted Pickle on the head and seemed to be asking him for advice. "Okay, but you guys jump in if I get lost, right?"

The waiter cleared our table, and we started for the Gathering House. Halfway there Pickle sat and told me and Kendra he was tired. She picked him up and carried him like a baby.

22

Once again we were arranged in the conference room. Kendra in the middle facing the seat waiting for Alexi. She'd arranged the props she used, notebook, pen, phone ready to record. I sat to her left, Henry to her right. Having my back to the door felt wrong, it had for the other interviews, but sitting in this order meant we had our subject blocked from running.

"I have ordered sentinels to wait outside," Destroyer said. "If this Alexi runs, he won't escape the imperial blockade."

I imagined eagles perched on the roof of the Gathering House like they'd done in the last case that The Inner Spell. I passed Destroyer's word onto the others, adding, "this feels different. I can't put my finger on why."

Kendra shrugged her shoulders releasing tension. "Maybe because we don't have any suspects left?"

"Be careful not to assume his guilt or innocence," Henry said. "My power is of no help, but if you stay neutral, we are less likely to be fooled. If he's innocent and we miss that clue, the real killer may take the opportunity to run."

Pickle who was curled up asleep in the corner whimpered. His feet made running movements. He's just dreaming I told myself.

"Ah, I see it's my turn," Alexi said cheerfully. "Shall I bring tea?"

He couldn't have overheard us. I'd put a ward in the lobby as we passed. His presence would have set off an alarm if he approached while we were talking.

"This shouldn't take long," Kendra said. She stood and pointed him to the chair. "We can have tea later."

He smiled and strode to the empty chair. Alexi readjusted its position slightly, and I noticed he was no longer directly facing Kendra. I wouldn't matter to her. If that little moment of control was important to him, let him have it. It didn't mean he was a killer, or he was innocent, just uncomfortable.

Kendra's emotions were locked down, but I noticed a little tightening of her shoulders. I looked over at Pickle, still well in doggy dream world, he would be no help in communicating with her.

"This is a terrible thing," Alexi said. "When I saw that image you gave us, Henry, I can't tell you how shocked I was."

"Yes, having proof of a murder is different, right?" Kendra said. "It's good, though. We know what we're dealing with. Imagine if we'd taken the word of the local police? We'd be back on Henbane, and Raven's Rest would have a murderer walking free."

Alexi paled at the thought. "Indeed." He turned to face me. "And have you found any clue to the identity of the person with that branch?"

I closed my eyes to rest my thoughts. I'd read every word through the lens of him being guilty without noticing.

These were normal questions. He was including me and Henry in the discussion and Kendra was doing a great job of dancing around the real questions. Making him comfortable. I was no use as an observer if I couldn't keep my mind open.

"We have more information. And perhaps a solid identification is only a few hours away," she said. "Tell me, why would someone wait until there were three protectors here to kill her? I mean, this was going on for a long time, right?"

"Oh what an excellent thought. Perhaps your presence was confirmation that Randi was endangering our world?"

Kendra made a noise of agreement and a note in her book. She picked up the book and flipped through the pages as if his words had jogged her memory. She nodded and put the notebook down.

"Who do you think might have reached the point were they thought the only sure way to protect the community was to kill Randi?"

"Let me think," Alexi said. He sat back in the chair as if relaxing would clear his mind. "I suppose someone she argued with might be a good starting point. Although that's almost every adult here."

"Can you think of anyone who Randi might have fought with not just argued?" Kendra asked. I could see her frustration at not just demanding whether he was guilty or not. She showed a lot of self control at sticking to the plan.

"Well, you have your list," Alexi said. "The council members. Yes, we were definitely at the end of our resources. We agreed I should call you in. Her roommates, Isobel and Quinn. You've talked to them. I think Maggie. But again she was on the list. Have to talked to Lela MacIntosh? She and Randi had ongoing professional disagreements. I'm sorry, I just can't think that badly of any of my neighbors."

We actually hadn't interviewed Quinn or Isobel separately. And Alexi was there for the joint interview. Perhaps we did still have some viable suspects. I suppose if you lived with someone who was so stubbornly intent on exposing your world, you might be the first to snap. I didn't get that kind of read on them, but maybe killing her had released any emotions. Guilt was the hardest emotion to read because we all had some little secret we regretted.

"What did the council try?" Kendra asked. "I mean, they must have tried to stop her before it got this far?"

"Randi was very hard to dissuade," Alexi said. "We tried to talk sense to her. Even though Felix said it wouldn't work, we tried blocking her from accessing the plain internet. Nothing worked."

Nothing he said was a lie. Kendra might not know what I saw in his emotions. He was sparking with conflict over an opinion he had. I decided this was the time to step in. "You have something else to say."

He gave me a smile and leaned forward. "I don't want to talk out of turn, but we did have some suggestions that I though would help. Ones we didn't try."

"What were they?" Kendra asked, picking up on my hint.

"Before I tell you, I want to say that I'm not blaming anyone for not acting. We don't like to restrict witches normally. I'm sure you are of the same mind."

"Yeah, no one likes to be punished for something they might do," Kendra said. "So what do you want? A promise we won't tell on you?"

No one needed my power to know she was losing patience.

"I see I've done my usual waffling," Alexi said. "I would prefer that you didn't name me as the source, but you are the protectors, I'll bow to your decision."

I was about to get up and use my power on him. Why couldn't he just spit it out? Henry caught my eye and gave his head a tiny shake. I took hold of my frustration and tamped it down.

Kendra just stared at him until he spoke again.

"We had several ideas. One that I thought was most likely to succeed was to put her under a ward charm. Just something mild that would make her uncomfortable when she though about going through with her plans."

"No wonder you didn't get approval," Henry said. "Control like that is forbidden for any reason."

Alexi gave him a hard look. "Even when a witch is foolish enough to risk the violent end of all magical beings? You can't believe the plain humans would welcome us? Your own vision showed that to be a fantasy." There was the passion he'd been hiding.

Forbidden magic was not an argument for today. I needed a lot of prep time to discuss the breaking of such a fundamental rule. Only one witch had broken it as far as I knew. Phillip. That hadn't expose us, but so many people suffered because of his actions.

"I think we'll leave it there," Kendra said. "You've given us a lot to think about. Thank you."

She closed her notebook and waited until Alexi left.

"Which one do you think we talk to first," she asked. "Quinn, Isobel, or this Lela person?"

23

Henry checked the list of contacts he'd requested when they started the investigation. "They have a land line. Should I start with that? Or would you like me to contact Quinn first?"

Kendra was cuddling the now awake Pickle. "Why Quinn first?"

"His name is first on the list of numbers," Henry said. "The council seem to have some ranking that only they understand."

"Does it matter?" I asked. "We can bring both of them, and interview each one separately."

"Oh no." Kendra said. "I forgot to ask Alexi if he is the killer. I'm so sorry. I guess he distracted me with all the new information."

We'd all missed that question.

"Maybe he's still here," I said. "I'll go look. You decide how to do the next interviews."

I hustled out to the lobby, but Alexi wasn't there. For all I knew he had an office in one of the wings. I didn't look forward to knocking on every door. There was no way I could pass that off as something innocent. I didn't want everyone thinking the protectors were frantically looking for the killer.

I checked the kitchen and the back garden. No sign of him. I pulled out my phone and checked the recent calls. There was Alexi's name. I hit call and waited. The call went to voicemail after five rings. I left a message and sent a text asking him to come back as soon as he could.

When I got back to the conference room, Kendra and Henry were still debating the order of interviews. We were all frustrated and lost. We needed to look at the case differently. "Let's step back," I said. "Alexi is out of contact for now. We can interview Lela first because we haven't talked to her. But we still don't know what Felix might have found on the SD card—it's been long enough for something to turn up. I think we also missed a key step. I apologize because I might have been too focused on training."

"How is Alexi out of contact?" Henry asked. "He just left."

"What did we miss?" Kendra asked at the same time.

I sat and sent a thought to Destroyer before I forgot him, too. "Can your spies find Alexi for me?"

"I will send their orders," he said.

Then I turned my attention back to the witches in the room. "I don't know how he could be out of contact. The animals will find him. As to what we missed, research. I would have D looking at backgrounds and history normally. We've just relied on gossip."

Kendra carried Pickle to the chair and pulled out her phone. "Yeah, and that's why I forgot to ask him. He controlled the information. And not just him, right? Everyone we've interviewed. We don't know if we've asked the right question. It's like all those shows I watched didn't teach me anything."

Oddly her emotions were optimistic. Henry and I were both dejected. I guess this is one of the situations were you learn from your mistakes.

"I have never run into this before," I said. "People lie, and we know when they do it. But something subtle like misdirection wouldn't trigger that power. I am so sorry, I should have been more alert. I'm a terrible teacher."

"There are three of us, Cossi," Henry said. "Kendra might be young but she should have noticed. And why did the protector power allow us to be fooled."

I hadn't even thought of that. "Good question. But a better one is what did we miss or ignore along the way. The power doesn't make choices like that. In my experience, it comes when the situation threatens our world. I can't use it for my own purposes."

"That's good, right?" Kendra said staring at her phone. "Like it would be really tempting sometimes. I don't remember ignoring anything, though. Except I guess I wouldn't right?"

"No, unless you were alert for it. I don't recall either," Henry said. "Did we rely too much on the power? Randi's death is not a danger to the world, in fact the opposite. The risk dropped when she died."

I'd always worked alone and thought that was enough. Having two different insights was new to me but today it was a huge benefit. "We will do some deeper thinking on this when we get back to Henbane, but I think Henry found the reason. Blindly expecting our role to make a difference is a weakness."

"Be that as it may, we have work to do. Starting with

Alexi," Henry said. "Let's find him and get our information before we go through anyone else."

"Nothing shows up on his social media," Kendra said. "I'm going to do some old fashioned searching. The oldies have more history than us kids and you never know what gets published."

I left her to poke around for Alexi's online history. "Henry, can you review all the interviews? Maybe there's something there to help."

He checked the time. "Perhaps you can speak to Felix? By now he should have more from the card, or know it's futile."

Good point and it made me think. "Do you think someone did what Alexi said the decided not to do to Randi? Put some wards on us? To keep us from solving the case?"

Kendra stopped searching, panic flooding her emotions. "On protectors? That has to be super illegal, right? More than just a regular witch. How would we know?"

Henry hadn't reach the level of panic yet, but he was definitely on the way. "I wish I had the powers to check."

"There's probably a spell somewhere," I said.

"You are not violated," Destroyer said. "The dog agrees about his familiar. The other witch I cannot tell."

I passed this on. Kendra confirmed Pickle's opinion.

"Then it is only me," Henry said. "I have no idea if I have misdirected you, or confused the investigation."

"You might not have," I said. "But a spell on you might affect us because we're close. Stand still and let me scan you."

A flash of fear tainted his aura, but he quickly suppressed it. "Kendra, hold my hand," I said. "We'll go in together. Maybe our combined powers will work better."

There was no stain on Henry's aura. No matter how deep we went, no trace of a control spell showed.

"Something has been deflecting us, but it's not a spell or charm." I let go of Kendra's hand. "Is it worth following up? Maybe something everyone in Raven's Rest has, or it's on the community? To keep the plain humans from being curious? That they wouldn't expect to work on us?"

We sat in silence for a long moment. My mind was spinning. Whatever I decided would feel it I'd been influenced.

"We finish what we started," Henry said. "Running off in multiple directions is not productive. My power can't tell us if someone lied, but I searched for answers to the choices. The best outcome was to continue our plan to research and follow up on the card. None of the outcomes were clear, that one was just the... better feeling one."

"I agree," Kendra said. "Like no one was around when you said we forgot to research. So no one was using magic to confuse us?"

"Okay. I'll talk to Felix."

Henry asked Kendra to show him where to search for background information and they both bent over their phones. I stepped outside of the conference room to call Felix.

"Ah, Cossi, did you see the message I sent with the recording?"

24

I stared at my phone screen. Don't panic. Maybe his package hadn't arrived yet. How would someone intercept it? I checked the reception area. No parcel or envelope addressed to me. I kept my voice even when I said, "there's nothing here. When did you send it?"

"About half an hour ago," Felix said. "I was a bit surprised when Alexi came to get it since you swore us to secrecy. But he's a council member, so I didn't argue."

There was no good reason for Alexi to intercept evidence, or to even know something existed. No. He had no reason to even think we'd found something because we didn't tell him we were going to search. Vijay wouldn't have told him. His promise to keep the secret was solid. I even after our discussion I couldn't come up with a single reason why Alexi would take the package... other than to get rid of the evidence he was a killer. One we couldn't find.

"I will instruct my searchers to double their efforts," Destroyer announced.

Felix was still waiting for me to speak. "Can you tell me

what you found? I'm sure Alexi will get it here, but it might not be a good idea to wait." I didn't want to start a real witch hunt. The only people who I trusted to find Alexi in one piece were already on the job. Yes, I considered Destroyer and his army people. He would find Alexi, it would all work out.

"Not enough, I'm afraid," Felix said. "As I put in my report there was a little more of the distorted voice we think is the killer. But the good news is, if I have recordings of the suspects, I may be able to match the voice. The computer is much more sensitive than our ears. That's why I use it instead of magic for all this technical stuff."

"You still have the card?" I crossed my fingers.

"No, that was in the package, but I have the recordings I made. That should be sufficient."

"Did Alexi ask what was in the report?" If he was the killer and learned Felix still had damaging evidence, we might have a second murder.

"I thought it best to keep my word about the secrecy. I hope that was right."

He hadn't made the connection that Alexi might be the killer, and he had the evidence in his possession. We needed to act fast before Alexi decided what to do with the information. I thanked him for his work, promised to send along any recordings we had and ended the call.

I returned to the conference room where my two protectors were still digging into any history that might help us find Alexi.

"Did you hear that?" I asked Destroyer. "The last bit?"

"I hear everything. I agree with your thoughts. I will... encourage my army to work even faster. We will find him. How shall we deliver him to you?"

I knew Destroyer heard my first answer: to the bottom of

the ocean. "Not that," I said because he congratulated me on my firm stance. "Here, to the garden. With no damage other than what you might need to do to transport him. And I need to know he's coming."

"He is rather large," Destroyer said. "It will likely be a forest cat, or possibly one of the local bears."

I heard the innocent tone. He was thinking, how can I be responsible if a bear decides to eat Alexi. "I will think less of your power over the empire if he is damaged," I said. "I think the best plan is to hold him in place until we can arrive because bears will be bears, right?"

"Correct. Not as much fun, but I will endeavor to fulfill your wishes."

My stomach growled. How was I hungry after that lunch? I checked the time. Oh, because lunch was four hours ago. I headed to the kitchen and filled a bowl with snacks—not nutritious, but filling. Tea went into an urn and then I headed back to the conference room. As short delay was better than trying to work without enough energy.

"We have something," Henry said as I entered. "He has posted in the past from a cabin quite near the Impossible garden."

Kendra held up her phone to show a photo of a cabin. "And he's got his phone on him, because he just posted that he's taking a few day to process a tragedy."

I dropped the sustenance on the table, told Destroyer the new information, and passed on Felix's news. "It's all circumstantial, but no matter how much I try to find another answer, I think everything is pointing to him as our killer."

"Then we should be able to summon him back," Kendra said. "Isn't there some kind of protector power we can use?"

"I wish. No, Destroyer has his spies out and we'll hear

something soon, I'm sure. Did anything you find have an audio track. I think that's the only way to know for sure."

"I'll look," Henry said. "If I find anything I can send it to Felix. If not, perhaps the council has recordings. We will catch him, Cossi."

"I recorded everything," Kendra said. "Like am I going to be this forgetful when I'm your age?"

"Send the files to Felix," I said. "We won't wait because, killer or not, Alexi needs to explain why he took the package."

"We should start working on a summoning spell when this is done," Kendra said. "It's stupid that we have to search for him. What if you aren't there the next time. I can only talk to Pickle and Henry doesn't even have that."

Not a great time for her to turn into the usual teenager. She was right. And I'm betting between Mrs. V and us we could find a lot of lost protector magic. And Pickle wouldn't be a puppy for long, and Henry might get a familiar. Too many mights and maybes to think about it now.

"Let's put that aside until we have this case resolved," Henry said. "Until we know for sure, should we keep this between us?"

"What are the chances the council will be able to help?" I asked.

Henry shut his eyes for a moment. "Unclear."

"Then we keep them out of it. The community has had too many shocks. I want to have the answers first before they learn one of the council members is a killer."

"Pickle says he can try to find him," Kendra said. "I think he's too young to go far, but should we try?"

I wasn't used to all the questions they thought I could answer. "I think we leave the real search to the other animals."

Pickle barked and then said, "I can help. I am rested."

Kendra ruffled his fur and reassured him he was a good boy.

"It might help to know where he went right away," I said. "I think probably Felix's place, although I have no idea how he knew there was evidence. We didn't say anything, even when he left."

"No," Henry said. "Kendra, strip the recording of its metadata and label it something innocuous. Then Felix can make the comparison with no preconceptions."

I reached for my phone. "I'll let him know you're sending it."

"Excellent," Felix said when I told him. "It shouldn't take more than a few minutes to see the results."

I didn't ask him if he knew why Alexi would know to pick up the evidence. If he knew he would have told me.

"Do we just sit here waiting?" Kendra asked. "I mean, I could do some spell research, right?"

"Perhaps we need to arrange a car," Henry said. "If he is in this cabin, we probably can't walk there."

My preference would be to get Mark here to help, but we couldn't afford the time it would take. "Can you drive?"

"Yes," Henry said. "You can't?"

"I have a license, but I don't like it. I never needed on in Vancouver, and cars are expensive to run and maintain. And Henbane is foot, bike, or sometimes horse. So, yes, but I don't want to."

I checked with Destroyer, but he had no update.

I didn't want to ask any of the council members because I still didn't want them to know. "We have a vehicle here," I said. "Let me find out if it's free."

A quick text to Mrs. V gave me what I needed. "One of

the shifters is in Sechelt. She'll drive up here. It will be nice to have another person on your team."

"And a shifter can make Alexi do exactly what we want," Kendra said. "Maybe she can join Destroyer's team when we go to the garden."

25

The shifter, Jeanne Vulpe, joined us as we were putting the final touches to our plan. As much as I wanted to run out and find Alexi, we didn't have enough information. Destroyer was still directing his army of spies with no success. That fact bothered me the most. Between the aerial and ground creatures there should be some hint by now. Especially when we told him about the cabin.

"You have directions?" Jeanne asked. "Maybe a shifter is a better tracker. Not saying your animals aren't useful. Dolph says they helped before, but they don't think like us."

If that was her being tactful, I'd hate to hear what she had to say when she was being honest. But she had a point. Destroyer could think things through, but he was only one crow. Most of the animals I met tended to forget the urgency when they were given complex problems. A shifter was another kind of human, she might think of a new way to catch Alexi.

"Shall I drive us to the garden?" Henry asked. "This

cabin must be near there. Even if he's not planning to stay, he'll likely have a, what do you call it? Oh, yes, a go bag."

"And if everyone and his dog knows about his hideaway, he won't stick around, unless he's stupid. I would really help if he is," Jeanne said.

As much as I didn't want to admit it, after so long, she was right. "Alexi's not stupid. And he's been gone long enough to grab whatever he needs from the cabin. If we don't find him, we might find a clue. Or if he's running, the animals will find him more easily."

"Well, what are we waiting for?" Jeanne checked to make sure we didn't need to grab any equipment and ushered us to the car. Pickle trotting beside her like she was his alpha.

Henry followed the route we'd taken on our visit to the garden with the council. He seemed to be keeping to the speed limit, but we arrived faster than I expected.

"Spell?" Jeanne asked. "Covering your actual speed?"

I guess I wasn't the only one to notice.

"A ward," he said. "Just a little 'nothing here of interest'. I wasn't going that fast anyway."

She grunted a laugh. "Check with your familiar, Cossi. Then I'll shift and go hunting."

"I can help," Pickle said.

Kendra passed it along to Jeanne.

"You would be an asset, little one, but your legs are not yet fully grown." Jeanne gave him a pat.

"I have not located the killer Alexi. The shifter is an excellent idea."

"Okay. Do you mean you haven't found the cabin?"

"We have found an interesting blank. Not like the ones on Henbane that other killer made. It took time for my subjects to notice, but an area where they did not enter. Sky or ground. When they reported, I deduced that it was wards."

I told the others.

Jeanne started removing her clothes. "I need a direction, or a smell, or a guide to get me there."

"I will send a bobcat, they are fast. Tell the shifter not to get into a fight."

Jeanne was already in wolf form. I picked up her clothes and placed them on the seat of the SUV. "Did you hear him?" I was never sure which animals could understand what and if shifters in animal form were like animals, anyway.

She spoke in my mind. "No. This form is only physical. I am still me inside."

I told her Destroyers instructions. Including the bit about fighting in case it was important. All this as we rushed along the trail to the garden.

"Tell the cat I will not eat it," Jeanne said.

"Are you sure?" A bobcat said as she stepped between a pair of giant hostas.

I spoke aloud so everyone knew what was happening, "You are safe. Take her to this warded place."

The cat and shifter loped away.

"So we just wait again?" Kendra asked. "And what is Pickle supposed to do?"

The puppy was staring off in the direction Jeanne left. I smiled at his eagerness, and hero worship of Jeanne. He was going to love Henbane. I added another task to my ever growing mental list. I'd take Kendra to meet the shifter Alpha, Dolph, when we were back.

"Can he sniff out any sign that Alexi passed through here recently?" Henry asked.

Pickle trotted off to sniff and mark the entire garden.

"What can we do if the wards keep even Jeanne out?" Kendra asked. "Like if he's got the wards in place, he might still be there. Why risk leaving when no one can find you?"

"I hope that's the situation," I said. "If he's gone, Alexi could be a the ferry by now. We might never find him."

A bird swooped by and landed on a branch of a plum tree. "The dog person is at the blank space. She says come now. Go through same path."

He flew away. I reached out to Destroyer. Why hadn't he told me?

"I am busy working with the shifter."

I corralled everyone, including Pickle who'd found a trace of Alexi's scent near the exit. "I Have found him."

Kendra picked him up. "Yes, a big treat is headed your way."

We slipped through trees and found a narrow trail. A little more than an animal one. Alexi must have passed through enough times to press the undergrowth down.

"Put Pickle down," Henry said. "He will find the way better than us. It won't be fast, but there is less of a chance we'll lose the path."

Pickle was wiggling in Kendra's arms. "Let me down!"

She put him ahead of Henry. "Find the shifter."

Much better than trying to find a blank space. Pickle's infatuation with Jeanne would get us exactly where we needed to go. And Jeanne would not have obscured the passage. I imagined Alexi had by tossing a few spells to cover his direction. They wouldn't last long, but he only needed a short time, anyway.

About ten minutes, thirty or so scratches on my face and arms and a lot of complaining, we stepped out to see Jeanne in human form. I should have brought her clothes with me, but she didn't seem to mind.

"I've tried to find the wards," she said. "But there's nothing right here."

"The blankness is a circle. There are no places where it is stronger," Destroyer said. "He has the source with him, and it is very powerful. Perhaps this object can be part of my imperial armory?"

"No."

"Fine."

Okay what do we do now? If we found the source of the spell, likely a small rock or a few of them, our protector powers could turn off the ward.

"This could be a distraction," Jeanne said. "If I was this Alexi, I'd make sure you couldn't follow me right away."

"Henry? Can your power tell us if Alexi is here?"

"It doesn't work exactly that way," he said. "Let me think."

He looked down at the ground and withing less than a minute, he projected three image circles. One was blue, one was red, and the other a deep mauve. I asked what they meant.

"It is most likely he is still here," Henry said. "See the saturation? The blue circle is the more vibrant. I think we pursue this opportunity."

I agreed mostly because we were here and if we walked away, I wouldn't know if it was our logic, or the ward that turned us away.

"As protectors, we should be immune," Henry said. "Why are we so affected?"

"It it's a general ward, that's true," I said. "This feels more tailored."

"Yes. He's had all this time to include our presence in the spell. Taking a teacup we'd used would be enough." Henry dug into his pockets pulling out notes, string, and a few acorns. "Sorry, I have nothing that will help."

Kendra took three of the acorns. "Let me try something."

I watched her concentrate on the objects. Her emotions fluttered between fear and determination. Then a slick of her determination covered the acorns.

"Sorry, I don't think I can make more," she said to Jeanne. "Will this be enough?"

"More what?" Jeanne asked.

"Oh, yeah I didn't say. So, I figured if we can't turn off the ward, maybe I can put a barrier on a ward to stop it from working."

26

"What will you do with them?" Jeanne asked.

"We just hold on each," Kendra said. "That will be enough for us to pass. I hope. I mean, that's what I told them to do."

"Then, I'll wait for you to come back, since I will not see what you will," Jeanne said. "It's a bit cold, so I hope you won't be too long."

"Go get your clothes," I said. "No need for you to freeze."

Henry handed her the car keys. "I'm sure you'll be back before we finish."

I hoped he was wrong. My main hope was that Alexi would just come peacefully and we wouldn't need Jeanne to guard him, or something more violent.

"I will assign cats and bears," Destroyer announced. "To act as bodyguards."

"Just little bears, please. We don't want him eaten." I imagined a giant Grizzly bear, although they probably didn't live around here.

"I see a building," Kendra said handing us our acorns. "Pickle stay close to me."

As soon as I'd taken the barrier charm, the ward disappeared. There was a clearly laid out and well-worn path in front of us, and as Kendra said, a small hut just within sight.

"We don't know if he's watching," I said. "Let's not dawdle."

We walked the path with caution. Or at least I did. I was leading and didn't want to turn my attention away from the hut to check. The fact we were headed his way, should tell Alexi we'd deflected the ward.

If he was inside, and if he was looking our way. His ward might have an alarm, or it might not. Alexi could be relying on its strength to keep anyone from even finding him.

The cabin was small but looked very much like a place he could hole up in for a long time. The roof and walls were well maintained and the forest would provide food, the Impossible garden was brimming with edible plants.

The first uncertainty was resolved just as we reached his door. It opened and Alexi stood there with a welcoming smile that had my truth detection sending off fireworks.

"Ah, you found me. I'm so glad." He opened the door wider and stepped aside. "Come in. I must say that taking time to absorb the events isn't as restful as I thought. I'm quite bored."

More lies. I didn't let it distract me. And Kendra would sense them too. "Did you pick up a parcel from Felix for me?"

He stepped over to a small table near the tiny kitchen area. "Oh, yes. I thought I would make sure there was nothing dangerous on it. Not that Felix would intentionally do something so awful, but times have changed."

Nothing he said had even a shred of truth. Did he really think we'd buy the idea Felix created a bomb, or included a poison in with our proof?

"Tell us what happened," Kendra said. "We know what happened, but the details make a difference."

She placed Pickle on the floor and he rushed to bark at Alexi. There were no words in the noise, he was too furious to tell me what he thought.

"I got the sudden urge to see Felix," Alexi said. "My magic sometimes works that way. I generally follow urges because they are never about trivial things. And this time it was a summoning to make the delivery. That's why I am suspicious of the contents."

"Stop lying. You know we can tell," she said. "Pickle come here."

The thing is, the last part wasn't all lying. Alexi had gone to Felix on an impulse. The whole possible danger was a complete fabrication.

"But, I." Alexi suddenly seemed to remember he was part of the council and forget that Kendra was a protector. "I will not be spoken to by a preteen in such a way. Cossi, get your student under control."

I glanced at Kendra. Here emotions weren't out of control. Her words were calculated. "Kendra is a protector. You will treat her as such. Her age is not important."

He blanched and sank into the couch. We were still standing, and it felt like we'd bullied him into submission.

"We know most of the story," Henry said. "Why don't you simply tell us what happened. Your actions require the appropriate response. Without your version how are we supposed to know what to do? Balance must be maintained. You know that Alexi."

Because Henry was talking, I had the chance to scan Alexi. Something I wouldn't normally be able to so without permission, but the protector power flowed into me. The scan had the flavor of protection so he was a danger to the community just for being him.

I retreated as fast as I went in. He was using compelling power, on all three of us. That should not be possible.

I thought back to our interactions. Surely I would have noticed if we were under his spell. Was I wrong about protectors being immune? Or was this compulsion targeted? It didn't matter in the moment, but we would need an answer later. I scanned again, looking for a way to counter the magic. No need. His spell was dissipating rapidly. The protector power sucking out the energy.

"You will stop trying to influence us," I said, the words seeming to come from someone else. Someone much more confident and stern than me. "If you do not do so voluntarily, I will impose a block on all your power."

Kendra glanced at me eyes wide. She didn't say anything, thankfully. I wasn't sure who was in control of my actions at the moment.

Alexi's emotions flared, and I thought he was about to attack me. Then they faded and drew into his core.

I wanted witnesses. "Henry can you turn off the ward?"

"Where is it, Alexi?"

"Under the sink," Alexi said. He put his hand over his mouth. "You can't compel me like that."

"And you thought that using a spell on us was acceptable? A protector can do a lot of things in service of the community," I said. "You must tell us what happened with Randi."

I felt the day brighten when Henry broke the ward.

Kendra went to the window facing the clearing. "They're coming. Jeanne is already back."

She opened the door then ducked. Destroyer swooped

in and landed on my shoulder. Pickle gave him a welcoming yip. Jeanne moved to stand behind Alexi.

"I can restrain him. Or you can cast a spell to make him come quietly," she said in a voice so neutral it felt like a threat.

"The story first," I said.

Alexi put his face in his hands and muttered to himself. It was too quiet for me to know if he was trying to cast a spell against us, or talking himself into giving up. There was no build up of magic, so I just signaled everyone to wait. We had time, it would be light for long enough that we wouldn't be walking a forest trail in the dark. Even if it did take longer, I could see a flashlight on an open shelf next to the small stove.

"I can peck out his eyes," Destroyer offered.

Saying no usually got me a lecture on being too soft. "First he speaks," I said aloud. "Then we can talk about eye pecking." I would not let it happen, but if Alexi needed a push, why not let him think I might?

He sobbed, and this time I didn't feel a lie in his defeat.

"It was an awful accident," he said. "I went there to try one more time to get Randi to see sense. We argued. She stepped back and I cast a spell to keep her safe. I still held out hope that she wasn't lost to her plan."

"If you cast a spell to keep her safe," Henry said. "Then how did she fall?"

"It went wrong," Alexi said. "I've never made a mistake with magic in my entire life. But somehow, possibly the stress, the spell twisted as I cast it. I watched it rush toward her. At the last moment it dissipated. It was so fast."

"So you decided to push her with that branch," Kendra said.

He hadn't lied, but I wonder if unlike mine, her power

could detect when he was lying to himself. We'd get into that on Henbane, and now I think of it, Henry should be able to tell a lie from the truth. How would a protector be successful without it?

I'd gotten distracted. I looked at Alexi. He was still attempting to influence me. Without thinking I circled him in a boundary to prevent his magic from reaching anyone.

"You saw Henry's magic," Kendra said. "We all saw that branch. Why won't you talk?"

Alexi was looking at me in horror. I guess he didn't know anything about protector powers. Of course, I was finding out a lot myself right now.

"I held it out for her to grab. I was going to pull her back. She thought I was going to push. She shoved it away. The movement unbalanced her and she fell."

Finally the real truth. Without his ability to touch us with his spells, Alexi had given up.

"Good to know you didn't plan on killing her," I said. "It is too bad you thought hiding your guilt was the best move. We need to go back to the Gathering House. Your council will need to hear the full story, and then we will all decide your fate."

27

Alexi didn't fight us on the way back. I wasn't sure if he'd given up or if he simply didn't have the energy to do anything. Jeanne's presence in her wolf form might have had something to do with it. But he walked head down and barely managing not to stumble. I did check his emotions, but they were muted to the point it was impossible to identify what he was feeling.

Kendra carried Jeanne's clothes and Pickle. The puppy treated us to a rambling commentary of the events until Kendra asked him to stop. The contrast between his cheerfulness and Alexi's depression was too grating for everyone.

On the way to the SUV, I reached out to Destroyer. "Are your spies still searching?"

"I sent them back to their usual activities, do you need me to find something else?"

"No. I just didn't want them still on the hunt. They did a great job."

"We were not successful in the first mission, but my army is talented enough to find the clue that helped."

He was right. I would remember that in the future. I

guess I'd been assuming they couldn't put two and two together when some animals were pretty smart.

We arrived at the car, and Jeanne shifted back to human. Pickle sat watching every move. I told him he wouldn't grow up to be a shifter.

"I know. I am a dog. I am the best dog. My witch tells me all the time."

"And she is correct," I said.

"I'll drive," Jeanne said as she pulled on her clothes. "Back to where I picked you up?"

"Yes." Where else? I wasn't going to take him to Henbane for a trial. That wasn't something we did. The remaining council members would be the ones to decide his fate because he'd put their community at risk.

"Then I'll drop you off and get on with my errands," she said. "Thanks for the side adventure."

"I'll let Dolph know you did a great job."

She nodded at me and a swirl of gratitude traveled through her aura.

"I will send a text to the council members," Henry said. "I think it would be better to leave the details until we are with them. I think it's possible Alexi had a partner."

He kept his eyes on Alexi as he talked. I hadn't taken my attention away from him even when talking to the familiars. The comment about a partner didn't elicit a response.

"Alexi, do you have anything more to add before we get there?" I asked partly to make sure he hadn't completely retreated from the world.

He took in a breath that hitched half way. "I have told you everything. I did not have a partner. This wasn't some well planned murder plot."

I didn't think it was. Now that we knew he was the killer, I recognized too many indications along the way. Not the least of which was the fact his name was raised by everyone we talked to as a suspect.

Jeanne parked outside the Gathering House and told us to call her if we were leaving today. "If you are hanging around, just call Dolph. We have the fastest boats."

I remembered the ride to Vancouver on one of the shifter boats. Fast, exhilarating and completely frightening. "I'll do that. Fingers crossed we'll be done before night falls."

She grinned, and it was all wolf. "Shifters can see in the dark. Don't worry about the time."

We walked with Alexi between us through the lobby. The council members were waiting for us there. A collective wave of surprise and shock went through them when they realized Alexi was a prisoner not a companion.

Kendra put Pickle down and told him to stay put. "We need a more private space," she said. "At least until you hear the facts. Then you can decide."

Marina stepped from the group. "We can ward the conference room. The Gathering House is built for transparency and community, so we don't have closed off spaces. We weren't naive, we knew there would be times for confidentially, so we created everything to be easily wardable."

We followed her to the glass walled room. When we were all inside, she asked, "will this part take long? Do we need refreshments."

One thing about witches that I loved was their need to feed people, not just kitchen witches, everyone. I wasn't in the mood to eat. It felt too celebratory, and this was not that kind of situation.

"Alexi, do you need anything?" I asked.

"No."

I scanned him, not deeply but enough to check if he

should have said yes. Just because I didn't sense a lie, I couldn't be sure he cared about his body.

"Perhaps some water," I said. "If this takes longer, we can bring in more substantial fare."

While Marina went to the kitchen, we sat. Felix took Alexi's arm and led him to the chair facing the door. He dragged another chair with him and sat holding Alexi's hand.

"I should have recognized the voice," he said. "I am sorry I did not, and I am sorry I didn't see how afraid you were, old friend. I'll sit with him if you don't mind."

I didn't answer. This was a good test of my two new protectors.

Henry spoke first. "It will be good for him to have a friend during this."

"We're not here to torture him," Kendra said. "Of course you can be with him while we talk."

Both good answers. I'd been here so many times that I knew it was useless to be emotional. That kindness went a long way without changing anything.

Marina returned. Put a glass of water next to Alexi and then the jug and remaining glasses on the end of the table. She turned and waved a hand to activate the ward and suddenly we were behind solid black walls.

"How would you like to proceed?" she asked.

"Alexi is your killer," I said. "You should take the time to ask whatever questions you have before thinking about his future."

Marina took the lead instructing the other council members to jump in when they had anything to add.

"Tell us what happened," she said. "All of it, Alexi. If you hold back, you may not have another chance."

Alexi told the story, and I watched closely for lies. Kendra did the same. Nothing changed. He told the truth.

When he was done, the council members were silent. Vijay filled our glasses and returned to his seat. They were all thinking and trying to absorb what they'd heard. I didn't read any doubt that Alexi was guilty. The shock of not knowing was overwhelming. That he took such a risk, and that he'd lost control of his spell.

Finally, Felix asked a question; not to Alexi. "Can you tell us if the original threat is gone?"

I turned to Henry.

He thought for a moment. "I can try. Do you need a visual?"

"Your word is enough, protector," Carmen said. "It was before. But thank you for showing us."

We waited while Henry consulted his power. Alexi didn't react, and that worried me. Everything that happened stemmed from Randi's determination to expose the magical world. "Marina, can you check Alexi, please. I think there is something wrong and you're the only healer here."

She glanced back at our prisoner and narrowed her eyes. "Yes, there is. Felix let me get next to him."

She placed her left hand on his heart and her right hand on his forehead. "You will not choose to leave us. You will survive to meet our judgment. Alexi, do not choose death."

Warm green healing power surrounded Alexi, and he opened his eyes. "You are right," he said. "I am not a coward. I will wait for your decision."

She returned to her seat and kept her eyes on her patient.

"The odds of this incident exposing our world are low," Henry said. "I think Alexi knows this and can explain."

Alexi, now much more present, said, "I found her cloud

account and erased all her files. That is what I told her that morning. That is why she was so angry with me."

"Any other questions?" Marina asked.

None of the council members spoke. As the protector, that last piece of information settled my mind that the job was done.

"It's time to talk about his punishment," Marina said. "Protectors, do you have suggestions?"

Henry and Kendra looked at me. They didn't know about the prison. It must be something only council members and protectors knew about. I was surprised neither of them offered a suggestion. Teaching them about punishments was another task on that darned mental list.

"There is the prison," I said, knowing the council must have heard about it.

"I think we want something more rehabilitating," Vijay said. "It was an accident, after all."

"You can choose no punishment if that's what you want," I said. "As the protector, my only role is to ensure your decision is not a threat."

"No," Vijay said. "At least for me, there must be some consequence. Yes, it was an accident, but Alexi made many decisions that led to it happening. I meant the punishment should not be permanent."

"It does not have to be," I said, remembering how we'd given the witches who Phillip controlled the option to return to Henbane. "The guards will take your instructions."

Vijay looked at Alexi and then back at me. "Do you think we can ask them to counsel him, and return him to us when he is... perhaps rehabilitated?"

"If that is what you want," I said. "My only recommendation is that we call the guards and have them take him before you tell the community."

"So we present them with a completed solution," Marina said. "I think we have our answer. Is everyone in agreement?"

The council voted unanimously for the solution.

I made the call and as usual the prison didn't waste any time. They must have guards out in the world ready to pounce on a prisoner—or they had some exclusive transporting spells. "The guards will be here by midnight."

"We will confine him in this room, but someone will be with him," Vijay said. "And, Alexi, if there is something you want from your home, we will bring it. One more question, if you will?"

The last thing I wanted to was get into a long conversation that kept us here too late. But I was the protector, so I nodded.

"The garden," he said. "Will we need to destroy it? There are so many plants we use in healing and, well, almost everything, it would be a pity to lose it."

I glanced at Henry who closed his eyes. Using the power was draining him. I think because of the barrier Kendra made. He didn't project any images for us; Vijay would have to take his word for it.

"The garden did not by itself pose a threat," he said. "Keep the wards, and perhaps create some explanation should someone stumble on it."

Relief turned Vijay's aura light blue—not just his. "I am so happy to hear you say that. May I create a small package of seeds and cutting for your earth witches?"

I very much doubted Raven's Rest had plants our Henbane witches weren't already growing. "That would be lovely," I said. "We are leaving as soon as we contact our ride."

"I will be only ten minutes," he said already running for the door.

I led Kendra and Henry back to our rooms. "Pack your things. I'll see if Jeanne can pick us up."

We were back on Henbane before night fell. Tired and needing time to reset. I sent a text to Valerie letting her know I'd drop off the package from Vijay. I also invited Mrs. V, and my friends to Jan's for a breakfast update before picking up Beulah from the bike parking.

28

The next morning, we sat at a table in Jan's bistro and told the story to everyone who showed up. Mark, D, Lilibeth and Mrs. V. We were the only diners at this time of the morning and Jan stayed at the counter giving us privacy.

"A sad thing, but still a good way to practice your calling," she said. "Allowing the council to make their choice was a nice touch. I think it's always smart to let other take responsibility for their community. What are your plans now?"

Trust her to ask the right question just when I was trying to work out the answer. What was I planning?

"I want to continue my training," Kendra said. "I still have four days before I have to go back to school. Then I can come back. I hope we don't have more murders. There are so many things I need to know."

"I too wish to continue to learn," Henry said. "Now that I can use my power rather than be used by it. I am happy to think of the future as a protector."

"I don't have some big plan, but I think training is the

best option," I said. "Training, but also figuring out what you both need. I guess more talking than formal learning."

Mrs. V stood, waved to Jan and said, "I will leave you to it. Cossi, when you have done this discussing, let me know how I can help."

This was so opposite the Mrs. V I met when I arrive that I couldn't speak. I managed a smile and a nod. Then she left, holding the door open for Destroyer to hop across the threshold and join us.

"I must meet this new familiar," he announced. "We were busy with far more important quests before. And a beer would be a good tribute."

"Too early for beer," I said. "And don't mess with Pickle."

He gave a very uncrowlike snort in my mind and hopped toward the puppy.

"BRING PICKLE OVER," Lilibeth said. "I'll check him over."

"I have to get back to work," D said. "The farm network is acting odd."

"I have a conference on Zoom," Mark said. "I'll come up later to visit."

At Lilibeth's it was the usual mixture of animals, some for daycare, some for long term while their witches traveled. Some animals healing from injuries.

"He's very healthy," Lilibeth said giving Pickle a cuddle. "I'll send up some food for him. Something special."

"What about when I'm home?" Kendra asked. "I have a leash but if he needs special food, where will I get it. And should he have toys? Special ones?"

"Don't fret, Kendra, I've got you. I'll send you regular deliveries of the food," Lilibeth promised. "Give him all the toys he wants. And exercise. Not just for his body. He needs toys that will grow this mind. This breed is very smart. You are very lucky to have him as your familiar."

Kendra picked out a few bags of treats and a couple of toys that required Pickle to figure out how to get those treats out.

The other animals in the shop sniffed the puppy or screeched a welcome. He was bouncing with joy at all his new friends.

"We should get going," I said. "I thought we'd talk and then go to Sheena's for lunch. Pickle can meet a lot of shifters."

"Wait for me." The voice came from behind the display.

I noticed that Henry turned at the same time as I did to locate the speaker.

A pretty tortoise-shell cat ran around the display and jumped into Henry's arms.

"Hi, you are my witch. I am Fearless."

PICKLE and Fearless settled on a blanket we placed in the kitchen. Lilibeth promised to send the cat food along with Pickle's. I sensed a little sadness in my friend at another familiar match. Not that she was unhappy for Henry, but she wanted a familiar of her own so much. I wondered if Destroyer could help. Maybe the right animal was too far away to find Lilibeth.

I pushed the tray of cookies toward Kendra. "Okay, let's talk about being a protector."

"Are you going to give us a grade?" Kendra asked. "Like if we get so many points we'll graduate?"

"I think, Kendra," Henry stepped in to answer for me. "That Cossi means what do we think a protector needs that we still haven't learned."

I wished he could be there to say just the right thing every time. "Yes. Henry is right. I don't really know how to teach you. It's not a job that comes with a strict definition. And when you are out there on your own, there's no guidelines, or rules, except the one. Protect the magical world."

"Do Henry first," Kendra said. "Maybe I'll get it by watching him."

That was a big step. For her to admit she wasn't sure. I'd seen her act like someone with decades of experience behind her, and also like the thirteen-year-old she was. I hoped she wouldn't be upset when we were finished.

"I think Kendra's spell helped me take a big step forward," Henry said. "Before she showed me how to control my power, I mostly hid away. As witch I was hiding in the plain human world at a job that mostly hid me from their world. Being able to live in the moment is something I've missed. Learning about the prison was useful, and I think, without being boastful, that I simply need to learn more of those types of things."

"There are probably some I haven't heard of," I said. "I'm not sure you need to know everything before you're official. You have me and Mrs. V to help. Other protectors when we contact them. Mrs. V thinks the best step forward is to make us a network."

"Like a secret society?" Kendra asked. "On our social media. Like the plain human WhatsApp thing."

"Not a secret society," I said. "That never works out well. But yes, like a WhatsApp. Where we can help each other."

"An excellent idea," Henry said. "And if other new protectors are discovered, they could be found and taken under the closest protector's wing until ready."

I decided to take a risk. "Henry, knowing that we don't know it all, how close are you to being on your own?"

"I don't think that's my call," he said. "You or Mrs. Vestum would know better than I."

"Nope," I said. "You will know."

He turned his head toward Fearless. "My familiar tells me I am ready."

"I think so too," I said. "We'll ask Mrs. V if she has anything to share, but Kendra is the one who opened your world."

He sat back and sipped his tea. The emotions surrounding him were mixed, awe, trepidation, pride, concern. "I cannot thank you enough for that, Kendra."

"Before you say it," Kendra said. "Pickle and I think we are not ready. Not just because I can't travel around the world as a kid. That can be solved with an illusion spell. I just haven't done much."

That was a weight lifted. "What would you have done differently? In Raven's Rest."

"Okay, now it's done, I kind of see why I would be wrong. But if I was in charge at the beginning, I would have pushed real hard. Maybe a light compulsion to speed things up. Now, I get that would be wrong. I'd leave the community mad at me."

There was that thirteen going on eighty Kendra. "You couldn't have compelled unless the protect power engaged. But your barrier power could have forced answers. Would Alexi have confessed if pushed harder?"

She thought about that for a while. Pickle didn't include me in the mental conversation so I just had to wait. The cookies were delicious, as usual. Valerie Nightshade didn't have it in her to make a mistake. Lemon and sage, not a combination I would have chosen, but every bite made me feel like I was home, safe, and comforted.

Two cookies later, Kendra finished her discussion with

Pickle. "I need a lot of training," she said. "Like I wish I could just go out and save the world, but I'd probably make things worse. I don't want to take like ten years to learn the job, though. So how do we make it happen fast."

Now I could offer suggestions rather than just tell her the facts. "I'm glad you learned so much. We can talk to your parents about spending your free time here."

She looked at her phone and then at Pickle. "I guess my friends can come visit? And I can keep in touch."

"What about your family?" Henry asked. "Will they let you come? I imagine they would like a claim on some of your free time."

She picked a cookie from the plate. "Maybe we can move here?"

I wasn't sure if it made sense for every family in need to move to Henbane, but it was a solution. "We need to talk to them, but not today. Why don't we take Pickle and Fearless for a tour of the island? Stop at Sheena's?"

A heat bloomed in my chest. Henry and Kendra both turned to stare at me.

"Another one?" Kendra said. "It's going to be really crowded here soon."

I had plenty of rooms, but having every new protector come to Henbane wasn't sustainable. "Henry, I think you should go to our newest protector. Mrs. V will know how to find them."

He thought for a moment. "Spain," he said. "I suppose if I found her, then I must train her."

WANT MORE

A quiet national park. A hidden magical community.
Reports of lights that drift away when approached and whispers no one can quite trace.
It sounds like exactly the sort of puzzle Cossi and Kendra enjoy solving—especially with their familiars along for the ride.
After all, how dangerous can a few wandering lights be?
Discover what happens next in ***A Miscast Spell.***

Use the QR code below to get your copy.

REVIEW

~

If you enjoyed reading Twisted Magic Casting, please consider helping other readers to find the story by using the QR code to leave a review.

FREE BOOK

Use the QR code to Claim your copy of Magic Will Out when you sign up for my newsletter and follow Cossi as she seeks answers to her past.

ALSO BY

For more books by Poppy Bridgeman

scan the QR code below.

ABOUT POPPY BRIDGEMAN

Hi, I'm Poppy Bridgeman, the cozy mystery alter ego of Canadian author P A Wilson. Poppy was "born" because sometimes stories need a gentler touch—with a little magic, a dash of humor, and plenty of sleuthing spirit.

As Poppy, I write the *Witch of Henbane Island* series (where witches and festivals collide with mysteries), the *EB Eats Culinary Mysteries* (a small-town diner, a determined heroine, and murder on the menu), and the *Pages & Paws Bookstore Mysteries* (a Devon bookshop, two mischievous corgis, and plenty of secrets tucked between the shelves).

When I'm not tangled in my characters' escapades, I'm happily tangled in yarn—I knit, weave, and doodle in sketchbooks between writing sessions. I also love to travel, finding inspiration for charming settings, quirky characters, and suspicious strangers wherever I go.

Home base is the Vancouver area, where I juggle writing as both Poppy and P A Wilson. Whichever name is on the cover, I'm always chasing the next story.

ACKNOWLEDGMENTS

Writing may look like a solitary pursuit, but I could never do this alone. I've been lucky to have support, encouragement, and inspiration from so many corners that it's impossible to thank everyone properly—but I'll try.

My writing groups keep me sharp and creative: The Vancouver Writers Social Group challenges me to see stories in new ways, The Royal City Literary Arts Society has given me the chance to learn from generous and talented writers, and The Other 11 Months group reminds me that words on the page are what really matter. My critique partners, with their sharp eyes and honest feedback, make sure each story is the best version it can be.

And of course, my heartfelt thanks to my beta readers. You catch the wobbly bits, cheer for the good ones, and remind me that these stories aren't just mine—they're meant for you, my readers.

www.ingramcontent.com/pod-product-compliance
Lightning Source LLC
LaVergne TN
LVHW050956080826
845145LV00009B/2320

* 9 7 8 1 9 9 7 9 4 9 0 1 5 *